This book is to be returned on or before the last date below.
You may renew the book unless it is requested by another borrower.
THANK YOU FOR USING YOUR LIBRARY

STONE CROSS
0121 588 2367
1 0 JUL 2009

1 6 AUG 2011

www.rbooks.co.uk
12244282

Also by Linda Newbery

The Shell House
Sisterland
Set in Stone

FLIGHTSEND

Linda Newbery

Definitions

FLIGHTSEND
A DEFINITIONS BOOK 978 1 862 30894 7

First published in Great Britain by David Fickling Books,
a division of Random House Children's Books
A Random House Group Company

First published in the UK by Scholastic Ltd. 1999
David Fickling Books edition published 2008
Definitions edition published 2009

1 3 5 7 9 10 8 6 4 2

Copyright © Linda Newbery, 2008

The right of Linda Newbery to be identified as the author of
this work has been asserted in accordance with the Copyright,
Designs and Patents Act 1988.

All rights reserved. No part of this publication may be reproduced, stored in
a retrieval system, or transmitted in any form or by any means, electronic,
mechanical, photocopying, recording or otherwise, without the prior
permission of the publishers.

The Random House Group Limited supports the Forest Stewardship
Council (FSC), the leading international forest certification
organization. All our titles that are printed on Greenpeace-approved
FSC-certified paper carry the FSC logo. Our paper procurement policy
can be found at www.rbooks.co.uk/environment.

Set in 12/15pt New Baskerville by
Falcon Oast Graphic Art Ltd.

Definitions are published by Random House Children's Books,
61–63 Uxbridge Road, London W5 5SA

www.kidsatrandomhouse.co.uk
www.rbooks.co.uk

Addresses for companies within The Random House Group Limited can be
found at: www.randomhouse.co.uk/offices.htm

THE RANDOM HOUSE GROUP Limited Reg. No. 954009

A CIP catalogue recard for this book is available from the British Library.

Printed and bound in Great britan by CPI Bookmarque, Croydon, CR0 4TD

For Liz, again

SANDWELL LIBRARY & INFORMATION SERVICE	
12244282	
Bertrams	08/05/2009
FML	£6.99
SX	

Contents

Part One

Part One

Flightsend

Flightsend arrived on their doormat, in an envelope from the estate agent.

'This looks interesting,' said Kathy, opening her letters by the toaster. 'Here, see what you think.'

She passed one of the printed sheets to Charlie. These arrived so often now that Charlie had stopped taking much notice. At first, she and her mother had read them all carefully, making comparisons, high-lighting important points; they'd visited countless unsuitable houses and had learned to read through estate-agent jargon. Even now, with the *Sold* notice in their front garden and the buyers waiting to move in, most of the printed sheets went straight into the recycling bin: too expensive, not enough garden, too big, too small. If a house looked promising enough for a visit, Kathy went on her own, always – so far – returning disappointed.

With each reject, each sheaf of papers to hit the bin, Charlie's hopes rose. Perhaps Mum would give up the idea of moving. They'd take down the

Sold board and stay here, close to the town centre, close to her friends. Close to the life she knew.

But the life they knew was the one Kathy wanted to get away from.

On Thursday, while Charlie was at school, Kathy went to see Flightsend.

'It's perfect!' she reported. 'There'll be a lot of work, but it's just what I've been waiting for. You'll love it, Charlie. Just wait till you see.'

They went together on Saturday, a raw autumn day that was more like winter, stirring memories of foggy mornings and afternoons dark by four-thirty.

'You'll have to navigate. These country lanes are a maze.' Kathy put the road atlas on Charlie's lap. 'Here.' She pointed at a tiny black cluster around a road junction. Lower Radbourne.

'It's a long way from town,' Charlie said doubtfully. 'A long way from anywhere.'

Kathy craned her neck to reverse out of the driveway. 'Yes! A real village. Pub, village shop, church.'

And what am I supposed to do for a social life? Charlie wondered.

She didn't ask. Mum would only remind her – as if she needed reminding – that GCSEs were looming, mocks and then the real thing. As they left the town and took a country lane between hedges, Kathy sat forward, her eyes scanning the road as if her perfect house, her dream cottage, might have moved itself closer to surprise her. Dried leaves clung to the beech hedges on either side; an open gate showed a muddy field entrance, rutted and puddled. Charlie saw horses sheltering in an open-sided barn and sheep huddled against a hedge. Ahead, a ploughed field rose to a line of tousled trees and an unpromising grey sky. Nothing looked very cheerful today, but Kathy was humming to herself as she slowed down and pulled over to the verge for a Land Rover coming the other way. The driver raised a hand in acknowledgement; Charlie glimpsed a peaked tweed cap.

'These roads are so narrow,' Kathy said. 'It must be difficult getting a coach round the bends.'

'Coach?'

'Coach. Bus. School transport,' Kathy said.

She's made up her mind, Charlie thought, before I've even seen the place. Well, I'd better decide to like it, then.

There was no one about in the village. The main street kinked at odd, awkward angles: a dog-leg by the pub, two sides of a triangle round a village green. Lower Radbourne consisted of one substantial Georgian house behind a gated wall; a pub, *The Bull and Horseshoes*; a tiny shop and Post Office with an OPEN sign on the door, and a scattering of cottages and small houses.

'Here's the church,' Kathy said. 'Norman, I should think.'

Charlie saw a lych-gate set in a hedge; farther back, gravestones and a sturdy building with a tower and an arched porch. Kathy turned sharp right down

a track beside the churchyard wall, then pulled up.
'This is it!'

They got out of the car. Charlie turned up her coat collar against the wind. The cottage, uninhabited for six months and wearing an air of abandonment, stood alone, sheltered by the churchyard yews. There was a tangled front garden, with a gate that hung lopsidedly from one hinge. Flightsend had blank, staring windows, and a porch that would probably collapse if no one did anything about it. *In need of renovation*, Charlie thought. And soon.

'What does it mean, Flightsend?' she asked.

'I don't know. Flightsend. Flight's End. Well, that's what it is, isn't it? An end to – well, to everything that's gone wrong.'

Charlie thought: I don't want ends. I want beginnings. The gloom of the place settled round her like fog. She thought of long winter evenings marooned here, miles from her friends. We'll be castaways, she thought, me and Mum. Flight's End was making her think not of settled contentment but of clipped wings, of pinioned birds.

'Perhaps it's to do with the old airfield,' Kathy said, shoving the wonky gate aside.

'But the house is much older than the airfield,' Charlie pointed out. 'A hundred and fifty years old, the blurb says. Aeroplanes hadn't been invented then, had they? Not even those ancient ones with wings that people flapped with their arms. How old's the airfield?'

'Wartime, I should think. Someone renamed the house later, perhaps. It's a nice name, anyway. I like it.'

But as for the cottage itself – Charlie couldn't imagine it as anyone's home, let alone *her* home. She saw only dilapidation and neglect. The house was perfectly symmetrical, like a child's drawing: the front door and porch, windows either side, two bedroom windows above; chimney-stacks each side of a tiled roof crusted with lichens. A weedy gravelled path led to the open-fronted porch and a door that had curls of paint peeling off; the nearest window showed a bare, gloomy main room that was probably full of cobwebs. Kathy stood smiling in the rain, not bothered about her wet hair. Her love-at-first-sight optimism was undiminished by cold wind and spattering rain. Charlie guessed that she saw climbing roses and honeysuckle, not dereliction and decay.

'It's perfect, isn't it?' Kathy said, turning to Charlie for agreement. 'I just knew! As soon as I saw it. And the name. It's just right.'

'But what about the inside? It looks like a ruin.'

'Of course it isn't. People were living here till six months ago.' Kathy led the way past the frontage to a yard at the side. 'Plenty of space, that's the really good thing. Just imagine, Charlie, when I've got it organized, with a little sales office, and signs up in the village and at all the road junctions. I can even do mail-order plants once I'm fully-stocked. Exhibit at shows, build up a reputation . . .'

Charlie saw ramshackle outbuildings that looked as

if they'd better be pulled down before they collapsed. An open-sided barn was full of junk – plastic sacks and what looked like rusty, outdated farm equipment.

'It'll cost a lot, won't it?' she said cautiously. 'Doing this place up.'

'Oh, well.' Kathy shrugged off the question as if money were totally irrelevant. She pushed through shrubs and wet leaves to the front door and opened it with the estate agent's key.

Inside wasn't much more inspiring. Dust, bare floors, an ancient strip of carpet that ran up the stairs.

'But look at the thickness of these walls,' Kathy said undaunted, slapping one. 'And there's nothing wrong with the plastering. Which bedroom would you like?'

The two upstairs rooms were almost identical, one each side of the central staircase, with a bathroom between – 'Look at the bath! Real claw feet. You'd pay a fortune to *buy* one like that' – and windows front and back. Each room had a fireplace with a mantelpiece, and the back windows, though small, looked over the garden, with meadows, beyond, sloping down to a tree-flanked stream.

'Oh, this is nice!' Charlie said, in the left-hand room that had an extra window at the side, imagining it curtained and carpeted, with her own things installed. The three windows gave the room an airy lightness, even on this dismal day. Bookshelves stretched each side of the fireplace.

'Good! You have this one, then,' Kathy said. 'It's the

first time you've sounded at all keen. I do want you to like it! It's just what I want, Charlie. More than that. It's what I *need*.'

Charlie hesitated. Would it be best to go along with Mum's new mood of sparky optimism? Or to deflate her by asking all the questions that came to mind? (Like: How are you going to make any money, out here in the sticks? What will we live on?) It was the first time in months – no, almost a year – that Charlie had seen her mother so positive, even excited; it would be mean to turn cynical. She tried not to think that this cheerfulness might be temporary, brought on by the new anti-depressant pills her mother was taking. They couldn't rebuild their lives on pills.

All the same, there were practical considerations that needed mentioning. She waited until they were in the car, heading back along the lanes, before saying, 'Mum, aren't we going to be a bit stranded, out there? I mean, you've got the car, but how am *I* going to get about?'

'There's the school bus. It stops at the village hall. I checked.'

'I don't mean just for *school*,' Charlie said. 'I mean – what about my social life? Unless you want me to join the Young Farmers, or learn maypole dancing?'

Kathy slowed to pass a horse-rider, who raised a hand in thanks. 'It's not that much of a problem, is it? You've got your bike, and I can always give you lifts to parties or whatever. Anyway, it's only another year before you'll be seventeen, and then you're bound to want driving lessons. Your own car, eventually.'

'Yes, but how can we pay for all that? Driving lessons aren't cheap.'

'Oh, I don't know. We'll wait and see. Things will sort themselves out,' Kathy said.

Charlie gave up. It was no good trying to reason with Mum, in this new mood of optimistic vagueness. She thought: this means so much to her. Too much. If it fails . . .

If *this* fails, too – then what?

She didn't want to know the answer.

February

Charlie walked down the stony track from the village hall where the bus had dropped her. A half-hearted fog had lingered all day; the school bus had its headlights on, even though it was only four o'clock, and mid-February, when the days could be expected to lengthen. Her bag, weighted with three lots of homework, pulled at her shoulder. Behind the yew trees at the end of the churchyard, Flightsend looked almost as unwelcoming as when she'd first seen it; there were no lights in the front windows, and the face it presented to approachers said *Here I am – like it or not, I'm not trying to impress.* And then, as she opened the front gate, Charlie's eye caught a splash of golden-yellow in the border by the hedge. Winter aconites, a drift of them. The first flowers must have opened today, above the frilled green rosettes of their leaves. Her mother, busy with cleaning and restoring the house and outbuildings, had found time to clear the overgrown garden, and now here were the aconites, floating like golden lilies on the dark soil.

11

They had waited underground all through the winter frosts, and now they were opening their petals at the first hint of winter yielding to spring.

Charlie wondered whether her mother had come out this way and seen them. They never used the front door. The kitchen was where they mainly lived, at first because it had been the warmest room in the house, and now because they were used to it. Charlie walked round the side path. Something else was piercing the soil in the dug border under the front window: something green and speary. Mum would know what it was.

Flightsend had been home for nearly two months now. To Charlie, it still didn't feel like a proper home. Home was their old house in town; home was family. And Sean. Now, it was just Charlie and Mum, and Charlie was finding it hard to adapt. This was how it had been before Sean came, and she'd liked it then. But now was different.

They'd moved in just after Christmas, in the coldest months of the year, shivering in the draughty rooms, and coaxing the Calor gas boiler into life. They got used to wearing bulky layers of clothing and two pairs of socks, and to using what Kathy called a sausage – a tube of fabric stuffed with old tights – to block the cold air that whistled under the doors. In January, while Charlie sat her mock exams, Kathy scrubbed and cleaned and painted, and got a builder in to repair the porch and the window frames. She got the ancient central heating system serviced, bought furniture cheaply at auctions, threw an Indian bedspread over the faded sofa and hung pictures. She worked outside, clearing the sheds, making space for her plants. She was tireless, always talking of her plans, looking forward to the day when she would open *Flightsend Hardy Plants*.

Charlie kept most of her doubts to herself. Flightsend was miles from anywhere and even visitors to the village could easily overlook it. There would be fierce competition from the big garden centres on every main road, with cafés and children's playgrounds and multicoloured displays of bedding plants; how could a small, specialist nursery, tucked out of sight in a remote village, hope to make any sort of income? At first Charlie and Sean, joining forces, had tried to talk Kathy out of what seemed a mad, impulsive scheme, trying to persuade her to keep her teaching job; but Kathy refused to listen to Sean. She pushed him away, out of her life.

Out of *her* life; but as Sean was a PE teacher at school, Charlie still saw him most days. She'd seen him today, in the canteen at lunchtime. At a time of year when everyone else was bundled up in sweaters and scarves, Sean was a conspicuous, athletic figure in a short-sleeved polo shirt and tracksuit bottoms. Even in winter his skin was tanned from the hours he spent outside on the sports fields. Catching sight of Charlie as she left the servery with her sandwiches, he came over to ask, as he often did, how Kathy was. Charlie always wanted to ask him, though she hadn't, so far: 'And how are *you*? Are you managing on

13

your own? You haven't met anyone else yet, have you?'

And beneath the casualness of his question was a sort of pleading that made Charlie want to tell him lies, give him the answer he wanted. 'She's falling apart. Come back. She wants you. We *both* want you.'

But all she said was, 'She's OK, thanks. Getting organized,' and Sean nodded and went back to the other teachers at his table. Charlie still didn't understand why Mum had rejected him, stubbornly choosing isolation and uncertainty. Sean was, in Charlie's view, the best thing to have happened to both of them since her own father had left, longer ago than she could remember. It would have seemed odd to call someone as young as Sean her step-dad, and in any case he and her mother weren't married; but nevertheless he'd been family for five years of her life, and now he wasn't. No one had asked Charlie how she felt about that.

She lugged her school bag into the warmth of the kitchen and found a gangling, skinny dog gazing devotedly at Mum, who was chopping vegetables by the sink.

'Whose is that?' asked Charlie, bending to stroke it.

'I don't know,' Kathy said. 'He just turned up, hanging round outside. Poor thing looks half-starved. I've given him some cereal and a bowl of milk, and I've phoned the police.'

The dog wriggled and tried to lick Charlie's face.

He was rough-coated, gingerish in colour and still half a puppy, with limbs not quite under control and an anxious, pleading face. He wore a collar, but no name tag.

'I'll get a bit of string, and take him round the village to see if anyone's lost him,' Charlie said.

'The kettle's on,' her mother said. 'We'll have some tea and then I'll shove the dinner in the oven and come with you.'

The fog had thickened as dusk fell, and there was no one about in the village. The cottage windows were lamplit and curtained. There were no street lights; Charlie found that strange, after years of living on a suburban housing estate. Radbourne House, opposite the church, had carriage lamps along its driveway and a sensor light that clicked on as Charlie and Kathy walked crunchily over the gravel. The plummy woman who opened the door said that the stray dog reminded her of a wolfhound she'd had as a child, but she'd never seen him before.

The dog walked obediently between Charlie and her mother as they worked their way round the rest of the houses. People looked at him sympathetically, but no one claimed him, or knew where he came from.

'The pub, next,' said Kathy.

In the *Bull and Horseshoes*, an elderly man drinking alone at the bar told them, 'I seen that dog a few times, hanging round. He been abandoned if you ask me. Lurcher, he is. Coursing dog. He prob'ly weren't no good.'

'Coursing?' Charlie asked Kathy outside.

'Chasing hares,' Kathy said. 'Two dogs after one hare. A so-called sport. Barbaric. They're gypsy dogs, aren't they, lurchers? Hunting dogs. Or poaching, more like.'

'I like hares,' said Charlie, who had seen a few out in the fields. 'Good for him, then, if he's a courser that won't course.'

'A lurcher that won't lurch,' Kathy said. 'We'll just try that other big house, shall we, the one round the bend in the road? Then we'd better go home before that casserole turns to charcoal.'

The big house was called Nightingales, a stone Victorian mansion that kept itself aloof behind high walls.

'Not that people in such a posh house would have a gypsy dog,' Charlie said doubtfully as they walked along the lane to the entrance gate. 'I bet some incredibly rich person lives here.'

'Oh, but look!' Kathy opened the gate ahead of Charlie, who had to wait while the dog cocked a leg against the wall. 'It's not a private house after all.'

Nightingales, said a large signboard inside the walled garden. *Residential and non-residential courses. Full programme of courses throughout the year.*

'What sort of courses?' Charlie asked, thinking of school. 'And what's the use of putting a sign there, where you can only read it when you're already inside? It ought to be out on the road.'

'We can ask,' Kathy said, but then, side-tracked, 'Just

look at this garden, Charlie! It needs taking care of, but *someone* knew what they were doing – look, *garrya elliptica*, and that beautiful prunus, oh, and hellebores with the snowdrops—'

'Come on,' Charlie said firmly, since her mother showed signs of disappearing round the side of the house for a full inspection. She marched up to the studded wooden front door and banged the knocker.

The woman who opened the door had short dark hair and was about Kathy's age, perhaps a bit younger. She was drying her hands on the striped apron she wore. Past her, Charlie could see a large entrance hall, with a reception hatch and a noticeboard; a table was set with wine-glasses.

'Hello!' the woman greeted them. 'Did you find your way all right? You're in good time, anyway. You can park in the stableyard, then I'll help take your bags over to the Well House. We talked on the phone, didn't we? I'm Fay.' She held out her hand.

'No, no!' Kathy said. 'We're not whoever you think we are. We've come about this lost dog.'

The woman clapped a hand to her mouth. 'Oh, sorry! I thought you were the Enamelling tutor. She's bringing a daughter, you see.'

Kathy explained about the ownerless dog, and Fay shook her head; then she looked hopefully at Charlie. 'You live in the village, do you? I suppose you're not looking for casual work?'

'Charlie's doing her GCSEs this year,' Kathy said.

17

'But I'd still like casual work,' Charlie said quickly. 'What is it?'

'Waitressing, helping out in the kitchen, odd jobs,' Fay said. 'I'm a bit stuck for tonight, to be honest. The usual girl's off sick and we were short-handed anyway.'

'Well, if—' Kathy began, looking doubtfully at Charlie.

'Yes, please,' Charlie said, completely forgetting about practical details like what sort of hours, and how much she would earn.

'Great!' Fay glanced at her watch. 'Gosh, look at the time. Can you start straight away? Oh – you'll need to wear a skirt. Black, preferably.'

'It'll have to be her school uniform skirt—' Kathy began. Then she stopped abruptly, looking into the entrance hall behind Fay. Charlie looked, and saw a little toddling girl, about two years old, in a red pinafore dress over a striped sweater. The girl came up to Fay and stood behind her, hugging Fay's legs and peeping out at Charlie and Kathy. Charlie was aware of Kathy's tenseness, her eyes fixed on the child.

'Oh, this is Rosie,' Fay said, smiling. She reached both arms behind her. 'Come on out, Rosie, you don't have to be shy.'

Rosie. Of all names. Charlie felt her mother receive it like a punch in the stomach. Rosie was a beautiful child, with brown eyes like her mother's, and hair brushed back under a velvet headband to fall in loose curls.

Charlie stood helplessly, her mouth opening to say

something polite. She couldn't think of anything. Kathy made a sort of gulping sound, pushed the dog's string in Charlie's direction, then turned and walked away fast down the path.

'*Mum*—' Charlie tried.

The gate clunked shut. The lurcher pulled on his lead and gazed alertly after Kathy, giving a faint whine.

Fay looked from the shut gate to Charlie, baffled. 'Oh, what did I—?'

'It's all right,' Charlie said quickly. Then, feeling like a traitor: 'OK, then – I'll just go home to change. Back in ten minutes.'

Rose

Charlie hurried after her mother, towed by the lurcher. He seemed to have accepted Flightsend as home and was pulling at his lead, his mouth parted in a grin. He knew his way round the side of the house, and pawed at the back door, eager for praise or food.

Charlie, fully expecting her mother to be upstairs crying in her room, found her instead in the kitchen, mashing potatoes.

'We'll keep the dog, shall we, unless someone claims him?' Kathy said, not looking at Charlie.

Charlie knew the symptoms. The blocked-up nose, the catch in the voice, the careful avoidance of the real subject.

'*Could* we?'

'It'd be nice to have a dog. Company,' Kathy said stiffly. 'And he's a good dog, you can tell. Kind-natured. Obliging.'

Sean's kind-natured and obliging, Charlie thought. Why couldn't we have kept *him*?

'You'd better go up and change,' Kathy said. 'Will you eat before you go?'

'No, there isn't time. I'll have it when I get back,' Charlie said, though her stomach felt hollow. 'Perhaps waitressing will make me eat less. Make me sick of the sight of food.'

'Don't be daft,' her mother said. 'I've told you before. You've got a large frame and you're a healthy adolescent and you need to eat. You'll never be stick-thin like those supermodels, thank God. There's nothing wrong with being well-built.' She served out a small helping of casserole for herself. Kathy's insistence on proper eating applied only to Charlie. During her breakdown, she'd got so thin that Charlie had been seriously worried about her starving herself. She was much thinner than Charlie, and at least two stones lighter.

Sometimes, comparing herself unfavourably with her best friend Rowan, Charlie made half-hearted attempts at eating less, but it was no good thinking that missing out on a few potatoes or abstaining from chocolate would ever produce a slim, graceful body like Rowan's. Still, if they were keeping the dog – she thought of taking him out for walks, of long-shadowed summer evenings out in the fields and down by the river. She could become fitter even if not slimmer.

'What shall we call him?' she asked.

Her mother thought for a moment.

'How about Caspar?' she suggested.

'Caspar. What do you think, dog? Do you want to

be Caspar?' Charlie asked. The dog looked at her and thumped his tail. 'OK, Caspar it is.'

'I'll borrow some dog food from Mrs Webster and get some more from the shop tomorrow,' her mother said. 'But we'd better not get too attached to him, yet. He might still be claimed.'

'There are other dogs. Now that we've decided to have one. We could go to a rescue place,' Charlie said.

But she wanted *this* dog, this lurcher, with his smiley mouth and his expressive eyebrows and his air of gratitude. He seemed to want to stay, and having him here made the cottage seem more like home, themselves more like a family. Three of them.

Upstairs in her room, Charlie forgot her hurry. She sat on her bed examining her fingernails and thinking about the life that could have been.

Usually she tried – hard – not to let herself do this. She had a new life now. This was what she had to get on with, and it was pointless to waste time thinking about the other one. But it was still there, penned up like water behind a lock gate, ready to flood out and suffocate her when she let it. Mum was the one who'd had the breakdown, but it was Charlie's loss, too. And Sean's.

None of them would ever be the same again.

They'd been a proper family. Herself, Mum, Sean. There would soon be a fourth person, when the baby was born. They spent so long waiting, planning. The latest ultrasound scan showed that she was a girl;

Kathy and Sean named her Rose. Sean and Charlie decorated the spare bedroom for her, choosing curtains and a wallpaper border with a pattern of chickens and ducks. Sean made a mobile and suspended it above the crib. A second daughter for Mum, first child for Sean, baby sister for Charlie. Their lives were all tied up with the future, with the date marked on the calendar. The end of waiting, the start of this new life.

Until.

Something went wrong. All the scans had shown a healthy baby; Kathy had felt her kicking. But her heartbeat faltered and stopped, and all the efforts of the obstetricians had been unable to save her. She died before she was born, and Kathy had to give birth anyway, to a stillborn baby.

Dead baby Rose. A life that never had its beginning. The nurses gave her to Kathy to hold; Kathy wept. They all cried together, Kathy, Sean and Charlie. Then, when it was time for the nurses to take the baby away, Kathy held on tightly, refusing to believe that Rose was dead.

Charlie would never forget seeing her mother leaving the hospital empty-handed, a few days later, leaning against Sean. The new baby clothes waited uselessly at home: the crocheted shawl and the Babygros and the tiny shoes. The empty nursery was a reproach. Everywhere she looked, Kathy saw emblems of failure. Charlie saw them too, saw her mother seeing them, and had no idea what to say or do. She could only think of the cruel disappointment. All those cells, splitting and dividing, making themselves into fingernails and toenails, lungs, eyes, a heart; all for nothing. Fate, or whatever controlled human fortunes, had played a callous trick. *You think you're going to have a baby, don't you?* it had teased them. *You wait. I'll show you.*

'Do you think we should do the room again?' Charlie asked Sean, when her mother was sleeping upstairs. 'Get rid of all the baby stuff, make it into a spare bedroom?'

Sean shook his head. 'That would be pretending Rose never existed. It wouldn't help Kathy, or us. You can't get over things by pretending they haven't happened.'

Charlie's grandparents came to visit, and Sean's parents from Staffordshire, and some friends. Others stayed away – because they didn't know what to say, Kathy said. Those who did come offered sympathy and comfort. 'You can try again,' they told Kathy. 'There'll be other babies.'

But Kathy only shook her head. No more babies. She wasn't going through all that again: the hope and the loss, the pain and the defeat.

'It's my fault,' she sobbed, when her friend Anne came round. 'I let her die. I couldn't hold on to her. I failed her.'

Charlie overheard snatches of conversation, round and round, over and over: her mother blaming herself, refusing to be comforted. Anne was the only person Kathy would talk to about the baby. She wouldn't talk to Charlie, nor to Sean. Baffled and hurt, Sean cooked meals for her, tried to plan outings to cheer her up. But wherever they went, they saw babies: healthy babies, beautiful babies, screwed-up-faced babies, in the street, in the supermarket. Babies kicking, crying, sleeping; babies with tiny fingernails and delicate tracings of eyebrows and whorls of soft hair; babies held by parents or grandparents. After a while Kathy refused to go out at all.

'It's understandable,' Sean kept saying to Charlie, always generous, always patient. 'She needs time. We all need time.'

But what Charlie didn't find understandable was that her mother was gradually dismissing Sean, pushing him away. At a time when she might have been expected to need him more than ever, she seemed determined only to hurt and reject him.

Charlie tried not to hear, but the bedroom walls were thin.

'You don't have to stick around with me.' Her mother's voice was tight, accusing. 'If you want kids, you can find someone ten years younger. Start again. There's no need to tie yourself down to a failure.'

And Sean's voice, quieter, insistent: 'But I don't want . . . Don't talk such rubbish . . . Why should you think . . .' And eventually, rising in angry despair, 'But I love *you*, Kathy, for Christ's sake!'

Charlie, at fourteen, felt that her life was falling apart. First, there was the loss of the baby sister she had so looked forward to; she'd imagined herself pushing Rose in a buggy, looking at picture books, reading stories at bedtime. The abrupt snuffing out of Rose, and of all the possibilities of her future, was bad enough. Even worse was watching her mother punish herself and Sean, dismantling their life together with what seemed to Charlie a deliberate, callous obstinacy.

Charlie had to do *some*thing. Eventually, after Sean walked out of the house one Saturday evening, with the strained, twisted-mouthed look that meant he was only just holding back tears, she confronted her mother in the kitchen.

'What have you said to him? It's not Sean's fault, what happened! Why are you being so horrible?'

Kathy was standing by the cooker gazing at a fast-boiling saucepan of spaghetti. They'd all been about to sit down and eat. She took no notice of Charlie, nor of the saucepan, which was about to boil over. Charlie snatched the pan handle and pulled it to one side, then turned down the flame.

'Mum!' It was like talking to a sleepwalker. 'Where's he gone? Don't you care that he's just walked out?'

Her mother turned away, studying the instructions on the packet as if she'd never cooked spaghetti before.

'*Mum* . . .'

Then Kathy said, slowly, 'You don't understand, Charlie. I know what I'm doing.'

Charlie stared at her through a cloud of steam. 'Upsetting Sean? Driving him away? Is that what you want?'

'Oh, for goodness' sake don't talk like someone in an American soap!' Kathy said, with a flash of spirit.

'But Sean loves you. He loves *us*. Why won't you let him help you?'

'Are you going to drain that spaghetti or not?'

'Yes, OK,' Charlie shouted. 'I'll drain the spaghetti and then you can sit down and eat the meal Sean's cooked for you. And I hope you're grateful. You won't even *marry* him—'

'No,' her mother said mildly. 'You're too young to understand, Charlie. He'll be glad, later. When he's found someone new. He's eight years younger than me and that's a big difference. He's not even thirty yet. There's plenty of time for him. I don't want to wreck his life.'

'But that's rubbish! You know it is. You *are* wrecking his life! Sean doesn't care about the age difference, why should he? Neither did you, till . . .'

Kathy shrugged. 'Everything's different, now.'

'Only because you're determined to *make* it different, to make it even worse than it is – oh, you're so selfish! Yes, you've had an awful time, everyone knows that. But what about Sean? What about *me*? You've got me, haven't you? Don't *I* count? Don't I mean anything to you?'

Charlie hadn't intended to shout, especially not these terrible *me me* things that made her sound jealous of Rose. But it was a relief to be yelling, words piling out of her mouth, an avalanche of the stored-up frustrations of the last weeks. Everyone had been stepping carefully round her mother as if she was a house of cards that would collapse in a heap if you breathed too hard. Perhaps it was time someone shouted loudly enough to rouse Kathy and make her realize what she was doing.

But Charlie had heard Sean trying, and should have known it was useless. Her mother seemed to have passed through some boundary to a place unreachable by logic, reason or any amount of emotional pleading.

'I know,' she said vaguely, 'and I'm sorry, but—'

'But what? Never mind *but*! Go after Sean and fetch him back! Do you really want him to go, for good?'

Kathy considered. 'Yes. I think I do. It's for the best.'

'Well, *I* don't! Mum, please . . .'

Her mother turned and stared at her coldly. 'Please don't harangue me, Charlie. It's not as if Sean's your father.'

Charlie was so infuriated by this that she couldn't answer at all, the words choking themselves off in her throat. She served the spaghetti, tipping it in careless dollops, splashing the sauce. She did three platefuls, putting one in the oven for Sean in case he came back. No, he wasn't her *father*; he was better than her real father, who'd cleared off when she was two. That didn't mean she wasn't entitled to care whether he stayed or not.

'I can't eat this,' her mother said.

'No, neither can I.' Charlie looked helplessly at the two plates, then shoved them in the oven

28

with the third one, just to get them out of sight.

Sean came back, and late into the night Charlie tried not to hear the discussion on the other side of the bedroom wall. She was frightened by this new version of her mother, this person who had shrunk deep into herself and couldn't be reached. Her mother had always been calm, organized, hardworking – above all, approachable. She had been good at listening to Charlie, talking about problems and uncertainties. Now, Charlie hardly knew how to speak to her.

Perhaps, Charlie thought, when she goes back to work, things will be more normal.

But Kathy had other ideas. A few days later she announced her intention of resigning from her Head of History at Charlie's school, selling the house and moving out to a village. It was her way of giving Sean a final ultimatum. Move out. Find somewhere else to live. The house was hers, not Sean's.

Charlie had another attempt at reasoning with her. 'But Mum! You *like* your job! Suppose you can't find another one? It's stupid to change *everything* . . .'

Kathy was in one of her iceberg moods. 'Changing everything is exactly what I want to do. Call it mid-life crisis if you like. I'm not going back to school. I've done it long enough.'

'But you were so pleased to get that promotion! And you've only *been* Head of Department for two years.'

'Doesn't mean I want to do it for ever. I've had enough of the National Curriculum and being blamed for everything that's wrong in the world. And of sulky teenagers. And their tedious parents. And classrooms and bus duties and spending hours each weekend on marking and preparation. There are other ways to spend my life, thank you.'

'But – what about *money*?' Charlie persisted. 'I mean, at least teaching *pays* you – what will you do without the money?'

Her mother gave her a scathing look. 'Do stop going on and on about money, Charlie. It isn't the most important thing in life, you know.'

'Perhaps not, but we still need it! What are we going to live on?'

'I've got that money my grandfather left me, from the house sale. Enough to get me started. It gives me the chance, Charlie, and I'm going to take it. Can't you understand? I need to make a change, and now's the time. I'm not staying as I am for another twenty years or more, working myself into the ground. If we can't manage – well, then I can go back to teaching. I've got to give it a try.'

Sean found himself a flat in town and moved out – Charlie wasn't sure she could ever forgive her mother for that – and the *For Sale* notice went up outside the house. Kathy devoted herself to gardening: digging, replanting, taking cuttings, tending her seedlings. Charlie couldn't see the point of all this garden improvement if the house was to be sold, but if gardening kept her mother sane, then gardening was what she'd better do.

They were on their own now, Charlie and Mum, and that was the way it was.

'Charlie!' her mother yelled up the stairs. 'What are you doing up there?'

'Just getting ready,' Charlie called back.

She tweaked at the black skirt that was a little too tight, and thrust on her shoes; then frowned at herself in the mirror, and clomped downstairs.

'Here's your coat,' her mother said. 'And take your scarf – it'll be cold later.'

She was finishing her meal, and Caspar was gulping casserole and mashed potato from a plate on the floor. Charlie giggled. 'I thought you said dog food? He'll be expecting this every day.'

'Just for now. He looked so hungry. Look, about this job.'

Charlie looked at her warily, thinking of the little girl at Nightingales, and Kathy's stricken face.

'Check what they're paying you, won't you? I mean, that woman Fay seemed nice, but you need to sort these things out. And about the hours. Don't take on too much, with your exams coming up.'

'OK.'

'And – I think it's a really good opportunity for you. Living in a small place like this – well, there isn't a lot to choose from. You'll meet people there. It might be fun.'

'As long as I don't pour soup into someone's lap. Or serve gravy instead of coffee.'

Kathy gave a tight smile. Once, confusing two jugs, Charlie had served gravy with cream and after-dinner mints to Mum, Sean and Anne. She could still remember Sean's incredulous expression when he was the first to taste it. For weeks afterwards he'd teased Charlie, asking for espresso gravy or one of her Bisto cappuccino specials. But incidents involving Sean weren't supposed to be mentioned now.

'Bye, Mum. See you later.'

Charlie pulled on her coat and scarf and let herself out of the back door. She thought: Well, I've got a dog and a job in one evening, and Mum doesn't mind – things are starting to improve. The three lots of homework in her school bag would have to wait.

Part Two

Frühlingsmorgen

Charlie watched the hand of the clock scything away the last sixty seconds of the Maths exam. Mrs Stapleton, the new Head of History, had been standing like a waxwork for the last hour; abruptly coming to life, she strode to the front of the hall.

If Charlie's mother hadn't left, she'd have been the one supervising the exam. This offputting idea made Charlie glad that it was no longer a possibility. At school, her mother had been Ms Steer, known to the pupils, inevitably, as Ms Steerious. She'd always made sure that Charlie was in someone else's History class, but nonetheless Charlie had had to get used to people making rude or disrespectful remarks about Mum in her hearing; also to the assumption (false) that her mother helped with her History homework. There were certain penalties that came with having a teacher for a parent.

One of the other History teachers, Anne Gladwin, was Mum's best friend, and that was odd enough. Charlie knew Anne both in her jeans-and-trainers, dog-walking, off-duty guise and in her teacherly role. Anne was on exam duty too; once, looking up from her paper, Charlie had caught her eye and they'd exchanged sympathetic smiles. Invigilating was what teachers hated most, Mum had told her: having to stand there doing absolutely nothing, when they had stacks of work waiting.

'Put down your pens. The exam is now finished.' Mrs Stapleton's voice rang out into the cavernous silence of the hall. 'Check that you've filled in correct details on the front of your script.'

Charlie directed a surreptitious grin at Rowan, across the aisle. That hadn't been too bad. One more done – three to go, with the weekend in between. What had once seemed an endless treadmill of revision and exams would soon be at an end; it was June, and this year's summer holiday would be longer than ever before.

Outside, she and Rowan compared notes.

'How'd you get on?'

'Not bad. Could you do the one about the vectors?'

'Sort of. Are you doing anything tomorrow?' Charlie asked, thinking Rowan might come out for a bike ride.

'Seeing Russell,' Rowan said promptly.

'What, all day?'

'Most of it.'

'Oh. Right. See you Monday, then. Or phone if you're not doing anything on Sunday.'

'Revising Geography.' Rowan made a gloomy face.

'Me too, I suppose. Well, have a nice time with Russell,' Charlie said, with only the faintest hint of an edge to her voice.

Rowan didn't notice. The mere mention of Russell's name, these days, was enough to bring a hypnotised look to her face. Charlie liked Russell, a tall, amiable boy, rather modest in spite of being brilliant at sports, but she couldn't help feeling resentful that Rowan let him take up so much of her time, with very little left for Charlie. Before Charlie had moved out to Lower Radbourne, she'd lived two streets away from Rowan. The two of them had been constantly in and out of each other's houses, especially at weekends.

'Why don't you ask her and Russell to come over one Sunday?' Charlie's mother had suggested, noticing Rowan's absence. 'You could take Caspar out, go for a long walk. A picnic.' It was the sort of thing Mum and Anne Gladwin liked to do.

'Rowan doesn't like long walks.' Anyway, Charlie knew how it would be: Rowan and Russell walking hand-in-hand through fields of poppies and long grass, gazing at each other, while Charlie was left with the dog for company.

Now she and Rowan stood in sunshine outside the main entrance, their eyes adjusting to sudden brightness after the shade of the exam hall.

'I'm waiting for Russ,' Rowan explained, as Charlie began to walk on. 'He had to see Mr Freeland about a tennis match.'

'Oh,' Charlie said.

Mr Freeland was Sean. Russell, who was in numerous teams, had a lot to do with Sean, for practices and matches. Football and rugby in winter; tennis, cricket and athletics in summer. Charlie wished Rowan wouldn't call him *Mr Freeland*. Before, coming round to Charlie's house, getting lifts in the car, Rowan had called him Sean. Mr Freeland made him sound like any other teacher.

Rowan took out a small mirror and scanned her face anxiously, smoothing a strand of hair into place.

'Don't worry, you haven't suddenly broken out in chicken-pox blobs or gone cross-eyed. See you, then,' Charlie said, and went over to her waiting bus. The sixth form had taken their customary places at the back, while the rest of the seats filled up with chattering kids from lower down the school. Charlie went to an empty pair of seats and sat watching Rowan, who had taken out a lipstick and was carefully applying it, regardless of her position in full view of the deputy head's office. *No make-up to be worn by pupils other than sixth form* was a rule that hadn't the faintest chance of being observed; all the same, Charlie, had she bothered to wear make-up at school, wouldn't have chosen to flout the ruling in quite such an obvious place. Then Russell arrived from the direction of the PE office, quickly making the application of lipstick pointless and breaking another of the deputy's unwritten rules: *No kissing or embracing on the school premises.* Charlie and Rowan had a theory that Mrs

Fortune (Misfortune, as she was known) made up these rules on the spot, to ban whatever anyone might want to do other than sit, silent and docile, in a lesson. Still, Rowan and Russell were a bit much, virtually re-enacting Romeo and Juliet's parting scene whenever they were separated for so much as one lesson. This time they'd been apart for a whole two-hour exam.

Angus David, a boy in Charlie's form, appeared in the bus bay, standing by her window and performing an energetic mime.

'*What?*' she mouthed back.

Angus signalled in more detail, something about catching a bus but going in a different direction now. Charlie had no idea why he should want to tell her this. She looked over her shoulder to see if he was gesturing at someone else.

'Hey, it's Aberdeen Angus!' yelled a cheeky year eight from the front of the coach. Angus, diverted, went into a new mime involving a bull and a matador. Then, as the bus pulled out, he clasped both hands to his forehead, pretending to fall over backwards, then sprinted off in the direction of the Arts building.

Oh, well. Angus was always play-acting. Charlie turned her thoughts to the two days ahead, a Rowanless weekend with nothing particular to look forward to. She was working at Nightingales on Saturday night and Sunday lunchtime, and would most likely end up helping Mum in between bouts of Geography revision. There was always work to be done, now that Mum had a limited range of plants on sale; the sign-board on the village green attracted a few customers at weekends. As the exams were nearly over, Charlie wondered if there'd be extra work at Nightingales. With no chance of a holiday this year, she might as well earn some money.

As the coach left the town, having dropped off most of its occupants in the surrounding estates, Charlie looked out at the fields and woods and the hills rising beyond. The countryside was in the full, unbelievable lushness of June, the hedgerows spangled with wild roses and elder blossom. The verges had been mown short by the roadside, but closer to the hedges there was a swathe of flowering grasses, ox-eye daisies and campions. Living in the Back of Beyond, as Mum called it, had its compensations. Later, Charlie thought, she'd take Caspar out, roaming across the disused airfield and down to the stream.

'Thanks,' Charlie called to the driver, jumping down outside Lower Radbourne village hall. Two younger pupils and one of the sixth form got off with her and the coach pulled away, taking the last trace of school with it. Exhaust fumes drifted away, leaving only the scent of honeysuckle and mown grass. Charlie breathed deeply. Friday. Weekend.

She walked slowly down the lane to Flightsend. Caspar bounded out to meet her, skittering through Kathy's reclaimed front garden. When Charlie had taken the brunt of his ecstatic greeting and wiped slobber off her hands and skirt, she found her mother in the lean-to greenhouse, potting up seedlings.

'Nightingales phoned,' Kathy said, after making the routine enquiries about the exam. 'Fay. She wanted to know if you could help out this evening – they're short-staffed. Can you phone back, she said.'

'OK. I'm not doing anything else.'

When Charlie came back outside after making the phone call, Kathy told her: 'I found something today, in the garden. Come and see.'

With all the nursery stuff to tend, more now since the polytunnel had been put up in the yard at the side, Charlie's mother had done no more to the back garden than pull up weeds. It was a glorious cottagey tangle of foxgloves, poppies, columbines and sprawling old roses, with bees foraging. In one corner was a heap of nettles and brambles, ready for burning. She led Charlie and Caspar down the irregular stone path to the end, where the fence caught the afternoon sun. There was a tall rose bush there, splashed all over with delicate pink flowers that perfumed the air.

'I was clearing a space underneath to plant a late-flowering clematis to climb through it,' Kathy explained, 'when I saw this. Careful, it's very thorny.'

Charlie stopped, smelling the rich, fragrant earth, and looked where her mother was pointing. It was a plant label, rather an elaborate one – not the usual garden-centre plastic but made of dark metal, with engraved lettering and a bevelled edge.

She turned her head sideways to see what it said.

'*Frühlingsmorgen 11th February 1988.*' She read it aloud. 'Nice name. It means spring morning in German.' German was one of her subjects.

'Well, I know *that*,' her mother said. 'It's a well-known shrub rose. I was wondering why someone had gone to the trouble of getting such a posh label.'

Charlie straightened and looked at the rose. She wasn't a great fan of roses, apart from the exuberant climbers her mother liked; but this one was beautiful, its starry, open flowers as uncomplicated as the wild roses in the hedgerows.

'It's a memorial,' she decided. 'A dog's grave, or maybe a cat. Someone buried their pet here and planted the rose bush in memory.'

'Caspar, what do you think?' Kathy asked. Caspar pressed himself against her legs and smiled up at her, wriggling. He wasn't in the least interested in the rose-bush.

'He can't tell,' Charlie said. 'No dog-messages coming from beyond the grave.' Oops! She was doing it again – amazing how often references to deaths, graves and burials came up in conversation when you were trying to avoid them. 'Must be a cat, then. Cat, Caspar! Can you sense cat?'

'It wasn't all that long ago,' Kathy said. '1988. Could have been the people who lived here before us.'

'I don't suppose we'll ever find out. Unless they come back to check that their rose is still alive.'

Another unfortunate phrase. Still, it was Mum who'd started on about roses, this time.

'Anyway,' she went on hastily, 'it looks great, to me. Totally thriving. You ought to sell Frühlingsmorgens, Mum, and people could come and look at this one to see how they turn out. Any customers today?'

'One. A hardy geranium enthusiast. She bought three – *macrorrhizum album*, *psilostemon* and *pratense asphodeloides*. And said she'll come back when she's made more space.'

'Oh, good,' Charlie said. She usually switched off when Mum started talking in Latin, but at least the dangerous ground had been circumnavigated.

She changed into the slightly smarter black skirt she'd recently bought for waitressing, took three biscuits from the jar – she would eat properly at Nightingales later – and walked round. Now that she was a member of staff, she used the back entrance, not the grander front one. Friday evening was always a busy time, with people arriving for weekend courses.

The back way led through a side gate and across the old herb garden, then into a walled courtyard planted with old roses. There was no one about, only Boots, one of two black-and-white cats. Charlie loved these glimpses of Nightingales without guests and busyness; the house and gardens had a quiet calm that she thought of as belonging to their Victorian origins. In an hour or two people would start to arrive, spilling outside. Charlie preferred Sunday afternoons, when the courses finished and the guests left, taking their cars and their loud voices with them, and Victorian quiet settled over the house again. She liked to imagine the house as it must once have been. All this space for just one family, with no doubt several maids, a nanny for the children, a gardener and a stable of horses. She saw the family having tea on the lawn, the women in white dresses, with parasols to shade their faces; it would be one of those long, hot summers in the years before the First World War. There would be a dog, a large dog like Caspar but more highly bred, lying in the shade under the table. If she'd been here then, she'd have been Charlotte the maid, not Charlie, bringing them tea, or cool drinks with ice from the ice house. Envying them their leisure and elegance, she'd bob a curtsey and go back to the kitchen, where she worked long hours for her board and a pittance. She'd be wearing a black dress that was too itchy and hot in this summer weather, and stockings, and a frilly cap and apron.

When she'd mentioned this vision to her mother, once, Kathy was amused. 'Why see yourself as the maid? Why not Miss Charlotte, the pampered daughter of the house, going to dances and garden parties and looking for a rich husband?'

But it hadn't even occurred to Charlie to think of herself as rich and idle. It seemed no more likely in the past than it did in the present.

A flagged path from the courtyard led to the utility room, walk-in larder and kitchen. Jon, who did all the cooking, was already stirring something in an enormous saucepan. Charlie knew better than to expect friendliness or conversation – he always became frantic at this early stage of a meal, giving curt instructions, darting about the kitchen on fast-forward. He was only twenty-five, and dreamed of being a highly-feared autocrat in the kitchen of a trendy London restaurant. Later, when desserts and coffee had been served, he'd award himself several glasses of wine, share a meal with Charlie and Suzanne, and wind down.

'Lettuce,' was all he said now, furiously grinding pepper.

Charlie nodded and fetched the box of lettuces from the store room. While she was washing them at the sink, Suzanne arrived. Through the sound of the running tap, Charlie heard her explaining to Jon: 'Sorry I'm late, it's just that I had to pick up Jason from the child-minder because Sam had to collect his car from the garage, you see it was having its full service and they hadn't finished on time because of a problem with the transmission—'

'Quiches,' Jon said. Suzanne, pulling a face, arrived at the double sink beside Charlie, with a sieve full of tomatoes to slice thinly for garnishes.

'Black mark for me. I should have known he wouldn't listen. The thing was . . .'

She went into a fuller explanation of her domestic problems. Charlie, only half-listening, said, 'Never mind. You were hardly late, anyway. What are the courses this weekend, did you see?'

'I did look at the programme. Creative Writing was one, and the other was Landscape Painting. One of the tutors was just going into the Well House.'

'Writer or painter?'

Suzanne giggled. 'Couldn't really tell. Could have been either. Anyway, he looked all right. *Very* all right.' Suzanne widened her eyes. She was always on the look-out for male talent. Just as a sort of hobby, she'd told Charlie; like window-shopping. The only man she actively flirted with was Jon, which was perfectly safe, since Jon lived with a partner called Andrew and wore a wedding ring with J and A entwined on it.

Charlie finished making up the bowls of green salad and went to lay the table. The long, narrow dining room had once been a library; it still contained shelves of leather-bound books and had a stone fireplace with a mirror over it. The guests and tutors – forty or so, when the place was full – all sat at one long table, which made serving the meals quite straightforward. While Charlie was fetching the laundered tablecloths and napkins from the trunk, Fay came in, wearing an elegant navy-blue dress and a slightly strained expression. She was holding a buttoned shoe of Rosie's.

'Hello, Charlie. I've got a favour to ask. We're fully booked for the next few weeks – it's marvellous really, but a bit much for Suzanne on her own. I was wondering if you'd like extra hours during the week? Your exams are nearly finished, aren't they? It'd be mornings, evenings and Sunday lunchtimes. Sunday

46

evenings off and all day Monday. Give it some thought – you don't have to decide now.'

'No, it's OK. I'll do it,' Charlie said. 'Apart from a couple of mornings the week after next, when I'm back in school for a sixth-form induction thing. But I can still come for those evenings.'

'Good! That's sorted, then. Tell Jon exactly when you can come and he'll draw up a rota. I want to ask your mother something, too. She does garden design, doesn't she, as well as plant-growing? I wonder if she'd do some work for us? The garden needs a good sorting-out, by someone who knows what they're doing. And we want to redesign the patio.' She waved a hand at the small terrace outside the library, overlooking a sloping lawn. 'Make more space for people to sit out. Perhaps have a pool. Do you think she might take it on?'

'I'll ask,' Charlie said, thinking: at least it'll earn her some money, but what about Rosie? How will Mum feel about seeing Rosie, Rosie's toys, Rosie's shoes?

Fay saw her looking at the red buttoned shoe she was absent-mindedly holding. 'Oh – I picked this up on the stairs. Rosie must be around somewhere with only one shoe on – I'd better find her. Ask your mum to give me a call if she's interested, could you?'

Once the guests came in, bringing the glasses of wine Fay served in the entrance-hall, there was no time for conversation. Charlie and Suzanne dashed in and out with starters, warm bread rolls, offers of second helpings, and tried to remember who'd asked for vegetarian, vegan or gluten-free food.

Charlie had occasionally helped out on Friday evenings before. These first meals, when people didn't yet know each other, were always polite and reserved, with conversational openers of the 'Have you come far?' and 'Have you been on one of these courses before?' variety. Charlie felt that her waitress role made her invisible; most people, apart from the odd word or smile of thanks, barely registered her existence. From this perspective, she found it interesting to watch the group dynamics over a weekend: to guess who'd be revealed as an extrovert by Sunday lunchtime, who the grumpy, dissatisfied one, who the gossip. At this stage, they all looked dull and middle-aged to her; most of Nightingales' clientele was her mother's age or older, with many of them well into retirement. Fay and Dan were considering offering Nightingales to school parties, but at present guests under the age of thirty were an extreme rarity.

Carrying a hot vegetable dish to the far end of the table, she was surprised by a youngish man catching her eye and winking. No, she hadn't imagined it; he was definitely looking at her, smiling. She did a double take, recognizing one of the art teachers from school. Mr Locke, Oliver Locke. Not her teacher; she'd been in Ms McGrath's class, but the art staff were a friendly lot, always drifting in and out of each other's classes to chat and to look at the students' work. Mr Locke, she remembered, had admired the still life she'd done for one of her exam pieces. Now, he broke off his conversation, and called out: 'Charlie! Didn't know you worked here.'

'Hello! Yes, just weekends, but more in the holidays.' She put down the dish and lifted the lid, releasing a steamy, fragrant cloud. She ought to be used to meeting teachers out of school, her mother's and Sean's friends, but it still made her feel awkward.

'Charlie's at Westbury Park, where I teach, for my sins,' Mr Locke explained to the people either side, who nodded and smiled. 'She's going to do Art next year, aren't you?'

'Well, I'm not sure,' Charlie stalled. She hadn't committed herself yet.

'Let me tell you,' Mr Locke said, 'that it'll be a terrible waste of talent if you don't.'

'What are *you* doing here, anyway? Are you—?'

'Tutoring Landscape Painting. I've known Dan and Fay for years. They've persuaded me to take on a fair whack of courses this summer. I'm staying in the most delightful cottage in the grounds. The Well House, it's called,' he explained to the guests. 'Come and see what's going on in the workshop, if you're around,' he added to Charlie.

She met Suzanne head-on in the kitchen doorway, balancing three plates. 'Hey! Just found out who it was you saw earlier – the Art tutor,' Charlie said in an undertone. 'His name's Mr Locke – Oliver Locke. He's a teacher at my school.'

Suzanne's eyebrows shot up. 'Lucky you, then. Can I join the sixth form?'

'Why wait that long? There's time for a quick enrolment in Landscape Painting,' Charlie said.

'Anyway, here's a challenge for you. Guess which one's the Creative Writing tutor? Female, I'll give you that as a starter.' Suzanne hurried on with her plates. She was very quick on her feet, in spite of wearing high-heeled, pointy-toed shoes which Charlie wouldn't have been able to walk in.

Serving the main course and dessert, Charlie surveyed the guests. For her and Suzanne, this was a regular game, identifying the tutors; Suzanne even kept the score. Charlie, so far, had proved best at bird-watchers and herbalists, while Suzanne specialized in long-distance walkers and bridge players. Jon was usually too busy to take part, but had once scored with an egg-painter.

'It's the youngish one with long hair and a floaty scarf and long silver earrings,' she told Suzanne, when the dessert plates had been cleared.

'Nope! Knew you wouldn't get it. It's the short, squat one with a tweedy jacket. I heard her introducing herself to Fay. Have a look when you take the coffee in.'

Charlie looked. The only woman who fitted Suzanne's description was stout and fierce-looking, with orange lipstick, and iron-grey hair pinned back in a bun. 'Of course most Rottweilers have super temperaments,' she was telling someone. That fitted:

she looked more likely, Charlie thought, to be running Dog Obedience.

When everything had been stacked and cleared away, Charlie walked home in the midsummer dusk. It was past ten, but difficult to believe that it would ever be really dark tonight. Upstairs, she opened her bedroom window and looked out. On some of the warm nights recently she'd seen a bat flitting after insects near the cottage eaves. The flicky, swooping shape darted in, too agile and too late for a bird, so quickly that her eyes couldn't keep up.

She leaned against the window frame, reluctant to go to bed. No bat tonight; but Frühlingsmorgen, spread against the back fence, called to her senses. Its flowers, like pale stars, gleamed in the twilight, and she could imagine that the warm air carried its scent to her even at this distance.

Runway

'I suppose it's too much to hope that you might sell barbecue equipment?'

The woman called across the yard as if summoning a servant. Charlie, who'd just changed into jeans after the breakfast stint at Nightingales, saw her mother come out of the polytunnel to explain that no, this was a nursery, not a garden centre, and that barbecues could be bought from the big place on the Northampton road.

'Oh.' The woman managed to convey, in a single syllable, weary resignation to life's hardships and the suggestion that she deserved better. 'Any bedding begonias?'

'No. I don't do bedding plants, only hardy perennials.'

The woman gave a tut but no *Thank you*, swished an irritable arm at Caspar, who was only being curious, and went back to the car parked across the yard entrance. She was just the sort of person, Charlie thought, to complain about the bad manners of the younger generation. Kathy greeted Charlie with a wry smile and brushed potting compost off her hands.

'Another one. I had one last week asking for garden furniture. I mean, isn't it *obvious*?'

'You'd think so,' Charlie said, placing her feet more firmly to avoid being knocked over by Caspar. 'There's a village fête next month, did you know? Fay and Dan are doing refreshments, at the house, and Henrietta from the shop is having a stall. *You* could have a stall.'

'Not if I have to do bedding begonias,' Kathy said.

She was wearing jeans and a loose, checked shirt and her hair was freshly-washed, gleaming coppery lights in the sunshine. Charlie looked at her, thinking, for the first time in ages, that her mother looked healthy, young, even *pretty*. Her face had lost the haggard look that Charlie had thought was here to stay. Her new way of life must be doing her good, regardless of tiresome customers.

'Shouldn't you *get* bedding begonias, if that's what people want?'

Kathy scratched Caspar behind the ears, making him wriggle and smile. 'Oh sure. Would you like me to sell gnomes with fishing rods, as well? I phoned Fay, by the way, about doing her garden. I said I'd go round tomorrow morning.'

'Yes, she told me.' Charlie had been surprised, relaying Fay's message over their early-morning mug of tea, by her mother's ready agreement. Perhaps the recent visits from non-connoisseurs were making her desperate for money.

'Oh, Rowan phoned while you were out. Not important, but could you phone back, she said.'

'I'm taking Caspar out first,' Charlie said. Rowan's offhandedness yesterday deserved a cool response. 'Coming? Or are you too busy?'

'I am a bit. You won't forget your Geography revision, will you? Now that you're doing this extra work at Nightingales.'

'I'm not likely to forget, am I? Don't worry. I'm devoting the whole afternoon to Urban Development and Land Use. Come on, Caspar! Walk!'

Caspar bounded ahead as she went to the kitchen for his lead. She decided on one of their favourite walks, along the lane past Lordsfields Farm and over the stile into the disused airfield. She knew from the local map that there wasn't really a right of way across the airfield, but she saw other people walking their dogs there, and no one seemed to mind. Caspar squirmed in anticipation as she turned into Lordsfields Lane. He loved the airfield, where rabbits grazed on the grassy edges, especially in the mornings and evenings. Charlie didn't think the rabbits were in actual danger. Caspar was so hopeless as a lurcher that he'd have little idea what to do with one if he got close; their bobbing white scuts as they dashed for cover made him leap about excitedly but without much sense of purpose. If he ever caught one, Charlie thought, he'd back off in alarm, or else give it a friendly lick.

Her spirits surged as she walked past the farm. It was

a perfect day, the early freshness giving way to the promise of heat. Placing her feet carefully, she smelled the sweetness of cow-dung where the Friesian herd had recently crossed from the yard after milking. Now the cows were in the meadow, knee-deep in buttercups. Charlie knew that modern farming wasn't as idyllic as it sometimes seemed, but when she saw cattle grazing by the willows that fringed the stream it was hard to feel anything other than deep, cowlike contentment.

She climbed the stile and watched Caspar dither – leap over or wriggle through? – before flattening himself into an undignified squirm, all the time looking up at Charlie's face for approval. A trodden path led to the airfield's perimeter track. Here, she let him off the lead and watched him trot off, snuffling in the long grass.

Charlie didn't know much about the airfield, only that it was in such a derelict state that it couldn't have been used for decades. The triangle of runways intersected a crop of barley. At the far end, where a lane led in from the road, there was a crumbling brick structure that could once have been a control tower. Farther back, in what was now a dense coppice, were the curved roofs of Nissen huts. It all made her think of old war films, black-and-white, with officers barking out, 'Scramble! Scramble!' and pilots dashing for the cockpits of their Spitfires. Those brave young men – not much older than she was – had taken to the skies to fight off enemy invaders. It seemed a war-film cliché now – the ultra-British accents, the heroism, the tragic losses – but nevertheless it had once happened. Happened here? Someone would know. Some of the pensioners in the village would remember. Might even have flown the aircraft themselves. It was hard to believe that the dashing young pilots in RAF uniform could now be as old as the leathery-faced men she saw in the village shop buying their newspapers and tins of dog food, but simple mathematics said that it was so.

She walked along the main runway, intending to go round by Devil's Spinney at the other end and make a circuit back through the village. The concrete was worn and corrugated under her feet, cracked here and there with grass and mayweed growing through. She could smell the pineapple scent of the crushed mayweed as she walked, and the air was so still that she heard each footfall, with a background of Caspar's snufflings, and birdsong from the wood. It was so peaceful here – there was almost, she thought, a timeless hush about the place – that it was hard to imagine the air disturbed by the clamour of aircraft engines.

And then she heard one. An insect-buzz in the back of her consciousness at first, deepening to a drone. She looked up, shielding her eyes from the sun. A tiny plane, mosquito-like at this distance, but coming closer, lower. Heading straight for her. For a few seconds her heart pounded and she almost dashed into the barley for cover, back in the war films again where Stukas screamed down on fleeing refugees. Caspar was barking, excited but anxious, his tail between his legs. Charlie realized that the plane was coming in to land; the runway wasn't the best place to be standing. She grabbed Caspar's collar, tripping over him as he tried to dash round her in a circle; the aircraft levelled out, not landing after all, but skimming low over the runway and flying on past. A light aircraft, white, with red stripes on the wings and tailpiece. No, she wasn't day-dreaming, or conjuring up some aerial ghost from the airfield's past; it was a real, modern-day light aircraft. Most likely the pilot was aiming for the flying club closer to Northampton and had made a mistake. Charlie felt rather ashamed at her panic, and was glad that no one had seen.

She released Caspar and walked on, thinking of a brief conversation she'd had with Mr Locke at breakfast. While most people had been tucking into the traditional egg, bacon and tomato, he was peeling an orange and drinking black coffee. When she'd said, 'Hello, Mr Locke,' he'd smiled at her and said, 'Call me Oliver, for God's sake, Charlie. Mr Locke makes me feel all crusty and school-teacherly and about fifty. If you insist on calling me Mr Locke, I shall call you Miss Steer. Good name for an artist, by the way.'

She hadn't understood that. Did he mean that it *would* be a good name for an artist, or that there was already an artist called Steer; or was he saying that *she* was an artist? She hadn't wanted to seem ignorant by asking, but the Rottweiler writing woman, next to him, had asked for Worcester sauce and she'd forgotten the remark until now. Perhaps Mum would know. When she'd told Kathy, with the early morning tea, about Mr Locke – Oliver – being a tutor this weekend, Kathy had woken up properly. 'Oh yes? Young Lochinvar?'

'Why do you call him that?' Charlie asked.

Her mother smiled. 'Anne started it. I hardly know him – he was appointed just before I left. But handsome young men are a bit of a rarity on the staff of Westbury Park.'

That struck Charlie as distinctly unfair to Sean, who was both younger and in her opinion better-looking than Mr Locke.

'He's not that young—'

'Sorry, you're right,' her mother interrupted. 'How stupid of me. He's positively ancient – at least thirty, possibly even thirty-one. How will the poor man manage without a Zimmer frame?'

'—nor all that handsome, as far as I can see,' Charlie finished.

'Have a better look, next time,' Kathy said.

Well, Charlie thought. If two of them, Suzanne and now her mother, lost their sense of judgement at the mere mention of his name – no, *three*, counting Anne – there must be something about him. She looked, covertly, bringing extra toast for his end of the table. Yes, OK, he was quite handsome in an unflashy sort of way: well-cut brown hair, blue-grey eyes, even features. And he had a *very* nice smile, like a light turning on and shining in your direction. She thought: I wonder if that's why Mum agreed to go to Nightingales?

No. She wouldn't run after Mr Locke, surely? Not after all the months of shutting herself away from everyone. Not when she could have Sean back. If Sean was too young, then so, surely, was Oliver Locke, only two or three years older. Charlie preferred to think that her mother was attracted to Nightingales by the offer of work, and the money. Mum would never chase a man. Her whole point, in breaking off and starting this new life, was to prove that she could manage without one.

Charlie entered the coolness of Devil's Spinney. A few weeks earlier it had been a haze of bluebells, the air full of their scent. By now the strappy foliage had collapsed limply, with dead flower stalks drooping. Whatever was supposed to be devilish about the place, Charlie had yet to discover. At first, Kathy had been uneasy about Charlie walking around the fields and woods by herself, but Charlie had argued that she wasn't alone; she had Caspar. However un-guard-dog-like Caspar was, few muggers would attack a person with a big dog in attendance. In any case, what mugger would choose to hang around a deserted wood miles from anywhere, in the hope that a victim might chance to come the same way? It was far more risky, Charlie said, to wait at the bus stop in town on a Friday night. Not altogether a wise thing to draw to her mother's attention, since any social life that came her way during the summer was likely to depend on buses and lifts.

She walked home through the village, and phoned Rowan.

'*Hi*, Charlie.' Rowan said. 'Come over this afternoon? We could revise our Geography together.'

'Oh? Why the change of plan?'

'I felt a bit mean yesterday,' Rowan said. 'You know, saying I was busy all weekend. It's ages since you came round, like you used to.'

'What's Russell doing this afternoon?'

There was a faint hesitation before Rowan said, 'Actually, he's playing in a tennis match.'

'Oh, I see,' Charlie said scathingly. 'Russell's busy so you're at a loose end.'

'*Please* come, Charlie. It'll be great. Dad's filled up the swimming pool.'

'I thought you said for revision?'

'We can't revise *all* afternoon. Bring your notes, though.'

'Well, OK then,' Charlie said. 'But I've got to be back here at six, for Nightingales.'

'I know,' said Rowan.

Cycling over, Charlie realized that Rowan had counted on that. The invitation was for the afternoon only; Russell would be available again by this evening.

Rowan's family had started off with a fairly ordinary semi-detached house but had spent enormous amounts of money on improving it. First an extension and conservatory; then the loft conversion, which was now Rowan's bedroom, with an en-suite bathroom; more recently the swimming pool. A garish shade of turquoise blue, it abutted the conservatory and took up most of the garden. Charlie blinked, dazzled by sunlight on water. The whole family was in the garden, on sun-loungers: Rowan, her parents, and Rowan's younger sister Victoria, who wore a crop-top and minuscule shorts.

'Budge up, V, and make room for Charlie,' Rowan said. Victoria, plugged into her Walkman, moved along one place, making a great show of reluctance. Charlie could hear the tinny *tssk tssk* of whatever she was listening to.

'Long time no see, Charlie!' Rowan's dad was loud-voiced, large-stomached and amiable. 'Let me get you a drink.' He actually had a poolside wheeled trolley, loaded with bottles and cans, glasses and an ice bucket. 'Coke? Iced tea? Fruit punch?'

'Punch, please,' Charlie said. She thought he meant home-made, with chunks of fruit floating on top, but it came out of a can.

'How's your mum's nursery business getting on, then?' Rowan's dad asked. 'I must get over there one of these afternoons and buy a few plants off her.'

'Great,' Charlie said. 'She'd like that.'

'Didn't you bring your swimsuit?' asked Rowan, who was wearing a slinky green one with high-cut legs.

'It's in my bike bag.'

Charlie never sunbathed; her fair skin burned easily and she was prone to freckles. Besides, nothing would induce her to lounge in her swimsuit in front of Rowan's parents, and supercilious Victoria, who by way of welcome had given her an indifferent stare; she'd have felt like one of those fat women on old-fashioned seaside postcards. All the females of Rowan's family were slim and beautiful, with glossy dark hair and smooth, unblemished skin. Charlie would put on her swimsuit for swimming, and not till then. She manoeuvred herself into the shade cast by a huge parasol.

Rowan's mother, having sat up to say hello, smoothed sunblock on her arms and legs and lay back, eyes closed. Rowan's dad flicked through the pages of the *Daily Mail*; Victoria was engrossed in her Walkman and a fashion magazine. It looked as if they were presenting themselves to the sun for the afternoon. They had all the paraphernalia of sun devotees: cushioned loungers, parasols, eyeshades. Charlie and her mother never did this; they always had something to do. They might sit on the grass to drink tea, but only before getting back to the range of jobs that queued for attention: young plants to be potted up and priced, labels to be handwritten, or the bathroom to be painted. Even before, if Kathy had sat in the garden she'd be reading some weighty book about the Russian Revolution or the House of Hanover. We're just no good at relaxing, Charlie thought. She couldn't just *sit* here. She felt twitchy and uncomfortable. She couldn't even really talk to Rowan, with everyone else listening.

Then Rowan's dad stretched, yawned, and said, 'I thought you girls were going to swim?'

'OK,' Rowan said. 'D'you want to go up to my room to change, Charlie? You coming in, V?'

'No, thanks. I don't want to get my hair wet. I only washed it this morning.'

'That's terrific, that is,' her father said. 'I spend thousands on the pool and she doesn't want to get her hair wet.'

Charlie's swimsuit was high-fronted with a racer-back, for serious swimming, not poolside loafing. Coming down from Rowan's room, she threw off her shirt and jumped straight in. The water was deliciously cool after her cycle ride, and the heat of the paved garden. She ducked under and surfaced, flinging back her hair.

'Ow! You're splashing me!' Victoria complained, flicking water off her magazine.

'Move further back then, whinger,' Rowan told her. She sat on the poolside, dipping each leg before lowering herself in. For Charlie, the pool was too shallow for diving and too small to do more than a few strokes in each direction. Still a little piqued with Rowan for using her as a Russell stand-in, she made the most of her swim, doing several proficient lengths of each of her strokes. Breast-stroke, front crawl, back crawl, butterfly – showing off, really. Rowan swam in a cautious breast-stroke, keeping her head above water and herself out of Charlie's way.

'You're making tidal waves!' Victoria complained.

'Go, Charlie! Someone enter this girl for the next Olympics!' Rowan's dad called out. 'I'm glad *someone* doesn't mind getting wet!'

Victoria tutted and moved her lounger to a safer distance. After a few more protests, she stood up, pushed her feet into sandals and announced, 'This is so *boring*. I'm going round to Trudi's.'

Charlie stopped swimming and leaned against the poolside, watching ripples dance as the water settled. Victoria clacked into the house, and her mother opened one eye to say, 'Hormones. She's just discovered boys, and how to be rude. She'll get over it.'

'Sooner the better.' Rowan climbed out of the pool and wrapped a towel round herself. 'OK, Charlie. Revision time. You can use my shower and I'll use Mum and Dad's.'

Charlie showered, and attempted to brush her hair out of its tangle. Every so often she grew impatient and threatened to have the whole lot cut off, but Kathy always talked her out of it.

'You've got fantastic hair, Charlie! Real Pre-Raphaelite flowing locks. Some people pay a fortune to get hair like yours. Don't cut it off, *please*.'

Charlie, not excessively concerned with her appearance, was never quite able to resist this appeal to vanity. Her hair was a curly gingerish mane, wild and unkempt, but if her mother thought it looked Pre-Raphaelite then maybe it was worth keeping. Charlie had discovered the Pre-Raphaelites last year, and saw what her mother meant – all those dreamy, other-worldly women, with hair like rippling fire.

She and Rowan spread out their Geography notes and textbooks on the bed. While Rowan went downstairs for more drinks and cake, Charlie selected Geology as the opening topic. However, Rowan had other ideas.

'I'm getting worried about your social life,' she announced, arriving with a tray.

'My what? It's on the list of extinct species. There was a last-minute campaign, but too late.'

Rowan put down the tray and passed over a large slab of lemon cake. Her own piece, Charlie noticed, was much smaller.

'Exactly. That's why I want to do something about it.'

Charlie sprawled on the bed. 'Really? What, you can spare time to unglue yourself from Russell?'

'Come on, Charlie. I'm serious. I feel a bit mean, especially now you live out in the Back of Beyond.'

'I *like* the Back of Beyond. I'm getting used to it.'

'That's just what I mean. You'll turn into one of those country types with green wellies and a loud voice. You'll end up marrying a sheep farmer. Or joining the Women's Institute, selling jam at the church fete.'

'Yeah, yeah. What are you planning to do, then? Pair me off with a Russell clone?'

'No. Well, not really.' Rowan licked the tip of her forefinger and dabbed up crumbs from her plate.

'What, then?'

'Persuade you to take a night off work at that Nightingales place. Come to Lisa's party next Saturday.'

Charlie thought about it. Lisa Skillett was in their form, not a particular friend of hers. 'She hasn't asked me,' she pointed out.

'No, but she will. And guess who's specially hoping you'll go?'

'Who?'

'Fraser. You know, Fraser Goff, in year twelve, who lives near Russ? Come on, Charlie, you deserve *one* night out, don't you?'

'Fraser wants me to go?'

Rowan giggled. 'Yes, he was sort of hinting to Russ. "Your girlfriend goes around with that girl with the hair, doesn't she?" is what he said. That's you.' She leaned over and tugged at a damp strand. 'The girl with the hair. Mind you, if he could see it now . . .'

'That doesn't sound like wanting me to go to the party. He could have meant "that girl with the *awful* hair", as in "Why doesn't she sort herself out?" '

'No, he wants you to go. He asked Russell to find out if I could find out if – well, you know. So that's what I'm doing.'

Charlie considered. 'So now, if I go, it'll look as if I'm only going 'cos *he*'s there? I hardly know him.'

'Just say yes, and stop making all this fuss. It's not like it's a blind date, or anything like that. We can just have *fun*. All our friends'll be there.'

'How'll I get home?'

'No problem. Fraser's got a car.'

Charlie looked down at her empty plate and realized that she'd eaten the entire slice of lemon cake, large as it was. She wasn't sure about committing herself to being driven home by Fraser. Still, it was a way of solving the transport problem, and Rowan was right – she *did* deserve a night out at the end of the exams.

'All right,' she said. 'I'll see if I can get Saturday night off. I'll *ask*. I'm not saying yes.' She picked up a sheaf of notes. 'Anyway, Geography.'

Feet clumped up the stairs to the attic room and Victoria stood in the hatchway, scowling.

'Have you taken my gunmetal eye pencil?' she demanded of her sister.

'No, I haven't! I haven't touched any of your stuff! Don't come barging in here accusing me. Anyway, I thought you were going to Trudi's?'

'She wasn't in,' Victoria said sulkily. '*Her* sister's taken her shopping.'

'Well, perhaps she's nicer to her sister than you are to yours!' Rowan retorted. 'Why'd I want to take *you* shopping, stroppy little madam? Why don't you go on your own, if you've got nothing better to do than trail round town?'

Victoria's lower lip jutted. 'Oh yeah, what with? The poxy amount Mum and Dad give me?'

Rowan laughed. 'Don't expect me to subsidize you. And remember I want my black top back. Washed.'

'Don't worry. I wouldn't be seen dead in it.' Victoria gave her sister a final contemptuous look, and clomped back down the stairs.

Rowan pulled a face at Charlie. 'That's the worst of this room. No door. People can come straight up without asking. V's getting to be such a pain. She used to be sweet, but these days she thinks she's the world's leading expert on anything to do with clothes, music, boys – you name it. It's always' – she put on a whining voice – '*What's that sad thing you're wearing?* or *What does Russell see in you?* or *How can you go out with your hair like that?* And she's so rude to Mum and Dad. You should hear the things she gets away with. *I*'d never have been allowed to. *And* she gets more pocket money than I got at her age, and does nothing to help around the house.'

'She'll get over it,' Charlie said.

'You sound like Mum. *She'll get over it*, and meanwhile everyone's expected to put up with Madam Mouth. Why should we?'

'All part of family life.' Charlie contemplated the idea that Rose might, one day, have been thirteen and stroppy. Whenever she thought of Rose growing up, she imagined her at two, three, maybe six – never as sulky-faced and pubescent. The Rose of her imagination was always sunny-tempered, charming and amenable – rather a lot, she realized, for anyone to live up to. Rose hadn't had to.

'At least you've *got* a sister,' she said mildly. 'And a proper family.'

Rowan's hand flew to her lips.

'Oh God, Charlie. I'm sorry. Foot in mouth.'

'Never mind.' Charlie brandished the sheaf of notes. 'Now, do you know anything whatsoever about Glaciation, and could you care less?'

Philip Wilson Steer

'You know the old airfield?' Charlie asked her mother. She passed a sandwich crust to Caspar, under the table.

'Mmm. Don't think I can't see you feeding Caspar. *Please* don't do that – I've asked you before. He'll start to be a nuisance when we're eating. I don't like it when dogs beg. It's undignified.'

'Was it used during the war? For fighters, you know, Spitfires, in the Battle of Britain?'

'Not very likely.' Kathy was making notes about propagation in an exercise book with *Westbury Park School* printed on the cover. She looked up, and straightened the glasses she wore for reading. 'The Battle of Britain was fought over Kent and Sussex, to stop the German bombers from getting to London. Northamptonshire would have been a bit of a detour.'

'But it does go back to wartime, doesn't it? The airfield?'

'Oh yes. Hasn't been used since, by the look of it. It was most likely used as a training airfield, this far inland. For bombers, I should imagine. As the war went on, there was more demand for bombers than for fighters. Most of the operational bases would have been along the south and east coast – Lincolnshire, Norfolk, places over there. Why d'you want to know?'

'Just wondering. When I was there this morning with Caspar, an aeroplane came in low, really low. A little light aircraft, one-man, I should think. I thought it was going to land on the runway.'

Kathy looked at her. 'And you thought it was a wartime Spitfire making an overdue landing?'

Charlie laughed. Caspar was pressing his face against her thigh under the table, and she hoped he wasn't slobbering on her smart Nightingales skirt. 'No! I was just wondering, that's all.' By now, thinking of the aircraft swooping low and the pounding fear that had almost made her dive into the barley stalks, she wasn't entirely sure that she hadn't dreamed it. She remembered the other thing she wanted to ask. 'Mum, is there an artist called Steer? Someone Steer?'

'Oh yes,' her mother said promptly. 'Philip Wilson Steer. An English painter, early twentieth century – a sort of Impressionist, I think. I've got a biographical dictionary if you want to look him up.'

'Thanks.' Charlie looked at her watch; she had to leave in five minutes. 'It's great to have a mum who knows everything.'

'I wish.' Kathy went into the sitting-room for the book, and came back with it open at the right page. 'Here he is. Philip Wilson Steer. 1860–1942. Yes . . .

influenced by the French Impressionists . . . leader of the English movement . . . known for seaside scenes. *The Beach at Walberswick* . . . Oh, I remember Walberswick, on the Suffolk coast. Do you? We stopped off there when Sh—'

Charlie looked at her. Kathy corrected herself. 'On our way to the RSPB reserve at Minsmere.'

Charlie knew what the unedited version would have been. 'When Sean took us to the RSPB reserve at Minsmere.' *Oh, great,* she thought. Sean's name can't even be mentioned now. She remembered that day: the shining expanse of water called The Scrape, the wading birds that you didn't see until you peered care-fully through binoculars. They'd seen avocets and a hen harrier and climbed steps into a hide that was right up in the tree canopy.

'And I went on holiday there when I was about ten,' Kathy continued. 'I think I've seen that painting too, the famous one.'

She passed the book to Charlie, who read the entry more closely.

'Why didn't you tell me? That we've got the same name as a famous painter?'

'Never thought of it, I suppose. We're not related, as far as I know. And I don't think he's all that well known. Not what you'd call a household name, like Picasso or Monet.'

'Yes, I think if my name was Charlotte Picasso, I'd have made the connection by now.' Caspar shifted his head, and Charlie reached a hand down to feel her skirt. Yuk! Her fingers met warm slobber. She stood up and tore off a piece of kitchen roll. 'Mum, do you think I should do Art next year, instead of Biology?'

'But I thought you'd made up your mind. You can't do Art just because of Philip Wilson.'

Charlie dabbed at her skirt and wiped dried mud off one of her shoes. 'Art was always the other one I might choose. Perhaps I'll do both. Some people keep four subjects in year thirteen.'

'Yes, but I don't think you'd better be one of them,' her mother said candidly. 'You wouldn't cope.'

'Thanks, Mum.'

'I'm being realistic,' Kathy said. 'You're a conscientious slogger – you wouldn't cruise through four A-Levels. People who do four are usually taking related subjects, like Sciences and Maths, not four entirely different ones. It'd be too much. You'd end up not doing well in any of them.'

Charlie humphed. *Conscientious slogger* sounded dull and worthy, far less exciting than artist, which was what Mr Locke had called her. 'Right, I'm going,' she said, pushing Caspar away before he could dribble on her again.

Her mother put a bottle of white wine in the fridge door; Anne was coming over for the evening. 'We'll talk tomorrow – you need to get it sorted out. What's brought this on, then? Have you decided Oliver's more handsome than you first thought?'

Charlie decided to treat this remark with deserved contempt.

'Have a nice evening. And don't get too girly and giggly with Anne,' she said, as her parting shot.

Mr Locke, however – she couldn't get used to thinking of him as Oliver – seemed to assume that she'd already made up her mind about sixth-form Art. He made her jump, calling her name as she crossed the courtyard. She hadn't seen him, in the shade of the wall, where he was sitting on the bench with a sketchpad and a glass of wine. The two cats were with him, Puss on the bench, Boots sprawling underneath.

'Sorry,' he said. 'Didn't mean to startle you. You looked miles away.'

Charlie had jumped because she'd been thinking about him as she came through the gate, and now here he was, as if her thoughts had conjured him up.

'What are you doing?' she asked, hoping he couldn't read her mind.

Dumb question; it was obvious what he was doing. It looked quite idyllic: the sunlight on warm brickwork, the climbing roses, the shady bench, the cats and the wine. He smiled and said, 'Hiding, really. I like these courses but it gets on top of you after a while, people always asking questions and wanting help.'

She moved closer. 'Can I see?'

He held out his sketch-pad. He was drawing the archway into the herb garden; a soft pencil sketch, with the detail of the stonework and a rambling rose; shade in the foreground, looking through into sunlight.

'That's lovely!'

He looked at her. 'No better than you could do, with practice.'

Yeah, right.

'I've found out what you meant, about my name,' she said. 'Philip Wilson Steer. English painter, influenced by the French Impressionists. Born in eighteen-something and died in nineteen-forty-something.'

'You've been researching?'

'My mum knew.'

'Steer's your father's name, presumably?' He had put down his wine-glass and was stroking the cat, caressing his head and ears and making him purr like a small engine.

'No, it's Mum's. My father left when I was two. He went back to Canada and I never see him. His name's Colin Cudrow. Mum and I were called Cudrow at first but when he left, Mum went back to Steer.' Charlie wasn't sure how much Mr Locke knew about her mother, or about Sean or the baby; whether it was common knowledge among the staff.

Oliver tried it out. 'Charlotte Cudrow. No, Charlie Steer's much better.' He wrote it in the air with his pencil, like someone signing a painting, with a final flourish. 'Charlie . . . Steer. Cudrow sounds like a line of cows in a milking parlour. Join me for a few minutes? There's wine in the entrance hall – shall I fetch you some?'

'I can't! Jon would go ballistic.'

'The temperamental chef? If you had one glass of wine?'

'If I sat out here chatting. There's a great pile of lettuce and tomatoes waiting for me in there.'

'You get time off during the day, though? Why don't you join my group tomorrow? You've got far more talent than most of these people, I can tell you.'

Charlie, unable to help feeling flattered, shook her head. 'I've still got exams to revise for. Geography and German. I didn't do as much as I meant to, today.'

'You'll have finished by next weekend, won't you? I'm going to be around, on and off, for the next few weeks. Portraiture next weekend; Life Drawing after that. It'd be a good chance for you to get some work in your sketchbook.'

Charlie knew he meant the sketchbook that formed part of sixth-form coursework. He smiled at her, relaxed and unhurried, leaning against the back of the bench. She was beginning to feel flustered – partly because she expected Jon to appear at the store-room door any moment and yell at her. 'But I haven't made up my mind yet,' she said. 'It's only a possibility.'

He looked at her seriously. 'Charlie, if you don't do Art, it'll be a criminal waste of talent.'

'Really?'

'I mean it. You'd do well, perhaps even brilliantly. With good teaching, of course.'

She looked at him sitting there on the bench. Yes, OK, Mum and Anne were right. He had the sort of face that grew on you, so that after a while you couldn't think why you hadn't noticed immediately what a good-looking man he was. He had an intent way of gazing at her that made her feel she was worth looking at. A shaft of sunlight fell across the arm that was resting on the side of the bench; he wore a white linen shirt with wide, short sleeves. Charlie looked at his shapely forearm, his hand resting on the curve of wood, and thought: I could draw that.

'I'll be late,' she said. 'No, I *am* late. See you later.'

Inside, washing, shredding and chopping the salad, she thought again about her subject choices. She had talent, he'd said; said it twice. Charlie wasn't used to being thought of as talented. Her mother's view, *conscientious slogger*, was shared by most of her teachers. *You have worked conscientiously this year* was a phrase that appeared often in her subject reviews. She took it to mean that she was quite unexceptional.

'You'd do well,' he'd said, 'perhaps even brilliantly.'

Brilliance, talent – the words danced in her head like taunting fireflies. Should she slog away at her academic subjects, or take the chance to do something at which – if he'd been sincere – she might excel?

She began to like the idea of herself as artist. The people who did Art in the sixth form were a group apart, more like college students (Mum said) than like school pupils; on friendly first-name terms with their teachers, drifting in and out to work on their projects or just to chat. The exam results were always exceptionally good, and each year several students went on to Art Foundation courses. Her existing combination of subjects began to seem less than enticing: each would involve hours of reading, essay-writing, sitting in classrooms. She would drop Biology. Pleased to have decided, she went cheerfully about her waitressing duties. When she went to his end of the table to serve the main course, Oliver Locke gave her a conspiratorial smile, as if it was all settled between them.

'Don't be too long,' Kathy said next morning, when Charlie fetched the lead from the hook behind the door. She was drinking coffee and flicking through the Sunday paper, having already changed from the faded jeans she wore for gardening into a smarter pair of trousers and a cream top. 'I said I'd go round at eleven.'

Charlie looked up at the kitchen clock. 'Why are you ready so early, then? It's only quarter past ten.'

Her mother gave an embarrassed laugh. 'Nerves, I s'pose. It's ages since I've been anywhere other than the builders' merchants or the supermarket.'

Charlie looked at her, noting the carefully brushed hair, the discreet make-up. Kathy hadn't worn make-up for ages.

'You're only going round for a chat,' Charlie said. 'It's not like a job interview. Fay isn't at all off-putting – you know that, you've seen her. And Dan's all right, too.'

In fact Charlie had rarely spoken to Dan, Fay's

husband, who was a musician. His eyes glittered behind round glasses and he had a beaky nose and a tangle of wiry hair, and looked to Charlie like a mad composer. (Gustav Mahler, Jon said.) He occasionally ran courses on madrigals and Early Music and tended to drift around the place humming to himself. He'd been introduced to Charlie, but several times since had passed her without noticing. He wasn't likely to intimidate Kathy. Charlie had the impression that Fay was the one who took decisions at Nightingales.

'I know, but . . .' Kathy looked down and turned a few pages of the newspaper, stopping at the gardening feature.

'Don't worry,' Charlie said more gently. 'I won't be long.' Her mother had asked her to look after the shop, as she was beginning to call it now that it attracted a trickle of customers.

Charlie whistled Caspar, calmed his excitable bounding and clipped on his lead. Kathy had been so engrossed in getting Flightsend organized, in setting up the nursery and planning for the future, that Charlie had almost forgotten this aspect of her breakdown: a tendency to panic about going out, meeting new people. The garden chat would be fine, but suppose Rosie appeared unexpectedly? Perhaps, Charlie thought, I should have warned Fay: asked her to keep Rosie out of the way. But that would have meant explaining the whole story, and she didn't want to give the idea that her mother was neurotic or unreliable. At least Mum *knew* about Rosie now, and wouldn't be shocked into bolting out of the gate. Charlie hoped.

Her feet took the way to the airfield again. There wasn't time for the complete circuit today, but she felt drawn to the place, in spite of the fear that had tugged at her yesterday. She passed the grazing cattle, the entrance to Lordships Farm; a man in overalls waved at her from the yard. On the airfield, she let Caspar off his lead and watched him leap away in great joyful bounds. Like a clumsy gazelle, she thought. From time to time he turned to wait for her, forelegs splayed, grinning. She could feel the corrugations of the runway through the soles of her shoes. It was a still, calm day with hardly a breath of wind. Already, the sun was hot on her neck and arms; she should have put on sunscreen, or worn a long-sleeved shirt. The buildings at the end of the runway shimmered in a blur of heat-haze. She turned and gazed into the sky. No light aircraft to disturb the silence today.

She felt almost disappointed by her mother's state-ment that no Battle of Britain fighters had flown from here. Just a training airfield. Still, in wartime it must have been a busy place, fenced with high wire, full of daily activity. Leading off the perimeter track were big cul-de-sacs of concrete, much overgrown with nettles and willowherb. Charlie presumed they were parking bays for aircraft. Bombers, her mother had said, not fighters; these concrete aprons were certainly large enough for big, heavy war-planes. How different Lower Radbourne must have been then, Charlie thought, with RAF people going into the pub for off-duty drinking, maybe billeted in some of the houses. The village had probably never seen such activity since.

'Caspar! Caspar!'

He'd found something. Nose down, tail up, he was snuffling excitedly at the ground, by the base of an ash tree at the perimeter fence. A rabbit hole, probably. She went over to look. She could see only one large entrance, not the network of holes and tunnels that rabbits made. She crouched to look. The soil in the mouth of the hole was well-trodden and there were dried tufts of grass and bracken that she thought had been thrown out from inside. Caspar was making small wuffing noises, pawing the ground. She held his collar to restrain him.

'Not rabbits,' she told him. 'Badgers? Let's not disturb them.'

If she came here at dusk, she might see one. She'd tell Mum, and perhaps they could come together, with Caspar if he could behave properly . . .

Then, gently pulling at Caspar's collar, she noticed something by the bole of the tree. A cross. A heavy cross, planted in the ground. It was made of iron, with flaking rust in the join of the crosspiece.

She reached out a hand. Solid, heavy iron, cool to the touch. There was no inscription, no clue to its purpose. It reminded her of the crosses people some-times left by the roadside at the scene of a fatal accident, with flowers left to wither and decay. No flowers had been left here; there were only the wild campions and cranesbills as a tribute to whoever had died here, or was buried here.

An odd place to die, she thought. Then she remembered that she had to get back promptly for her mother.

'Come on, Caspar. We can't be late.'

Glancing at her watch, she took the shorter way back past Hog Pond, crossing a stile from the perimeter track and through the thistly field that lay behind the Post Office and shop. The pond was near the airfield fence, rather dank and smelly, fringed with willows. Charlie, who knew the name from the map, liked to imagine a medieval pig farm just here, with bristly brown pigs, rather than modern pink ones, snorting and rooting, and wallowing in the mud of the pond. Caspar snuffled along the hedgerow, smelling rabbits, his back end wriggling comically. There was a big sign-board just inside the gate, blank on the side nearest Charlie, facing the narrow lane that led down beside the Post Office. She hadn't seen it before, and the clayey soil around its posts looked newly disturbed.

'Caspar! Here! *Good* boy.'

She clipped his lead on, then turned to see what the board was for.

Honeysuckle Coppice, it said. *A development of 12 superior detached country homes.*

'This is our last Sunday lunch together, do you realize?' Charlie said. 'From now on I'll be up at

Nightingales. So it went well, then, your meeting?'

'Oh yes! Pass the rice salad, I'm starving.'

Charlie watched with approval as her mother took a quite reasonable-sized helping.

'We had a chat,' Kathy went on, 'and we had coffee, and I sketched out a few rough ideas. I'm going to draw up more detailed plans and then go back to show them. They're nice, aren't they, Fay and Dan?'

She didn't mention Rosie.

'And did you see Oliver Heart-throb Locke while you were there?' Charlie asked innocently.

'Yes, I did actually.' Kathy gave Charlie a searching look. 'He said how pleased he was you're doing Art next year, and that he's sure you'll do well. I didn't realize you'd been discussing it with him.'

'Well, not really. He just sort of *assumes*. But I've been thinking about it, Mum, and I really do want to do it. *Not* because of him. Because I want to.'

Her mother nodded. 'Make sure you tell Ms Winterbourne in time for the induction course, then.' Ms Winterbourne was the Head of Sixth Form. 'Anyway, it's not written in stone, even then. People keep changing their minds right up till September. Even *after* September, sometimes.'

'OK.' Surprised that it had been so easy, Charlie went on, 'I sold some plants! Two Jacob's Ladder, one French lavender, one penstemon. Wasn't that good? To the people from Radbourne House. And they took one of your plant lists and said they'd come back. Oh, but Mum, I found out something awful –

there are going to be new houses built in the field behind the Post Office! *Honeysuckle Coppice,* of all names.'

Kathy was less perturbed than she expected. 'Well, it happens. You've only got to look at the other villages round here. People need to live somewhere.'

'Yes, I know, but – so close to the airfield – I suppose *that*'ll be built on next, and the bluebell wood! Oh, Mum, it'll be awful!'

'Have some salad.' Kathy passed the bowl.

'I can hardly look a lettuce leaf in the face,' Charlie said, but took some anyway. 'There are badgers on the airfield! I think so, anyway. I saw a sett.'

Coming across the builders' board had pushed the discovery of the cross out of her head. Remembering now, she told her mother about it.

'Odd, don't you think? I mean, who could have died there? Or been buried there? Do you think it might go back to wartime, to when the airfield was used? But it's not like a proper war memorial. There's no name on it, nothing.'

'Mmm.' Her mother passed a bowl of cherry tomatoes. 'Have some of these.'

'And you said it was a training airfield. So people wouldn't have been likely to kill themselves flying, would they? It's not like one of those Battle of Britain places you were talking about, with dog-fights going on every day.'

'It's *highly* likely that people killed themselves flying,' Kathy said. 'In fact I should think it's the most likely explanation. There was a high casualty rate, especially in the early years of the war. Training accidents happened all the time. The aircraft didn't have sophisticated navigation devices, at first. There were all sorts of fatal accidents with pilots trying to land in fog, or just getting lost. *Terrible* losses, the aircrew had. More than fifty thousand, in all.'

'I don't suppose we'll ever know,' Charlie said. 'Especially if the whole airfield gets ripped up to make room for a new housing estate.'

Her mother looked amused. 'It's not a question of the whole airfield, yet! Aren't you being a bit NIMBY about this – you know, *not in my back yard*?'

'No! Oh, I don't know. Yes!'

'Twelve new houses won't ruin the village,' Kathy said. 'And you can't blame farmers for selling off land. Just think of the time they've had, with foot-and-mouth, and drought, and floods, and cheaper food coming in from Europe. Wouldn't *you* take the chance of making a few hundred thousand pounds, and retiring on the proceeds?'

'But it's just the start! Those houses will back right on to the airfield, and then what's going to stop someone putting up another twenty, or forty, or a hundred?'

Kathy looked at her. 'Why are you so attached to that airfield? There are other places you can walk Caspar.'

'Yes, I know, but – well, it's history! Part of the village's past. You're a historian, you must feel the same.' Charlie looked at the last piece of baguette, thought of her weight, and took it anyway.

'But almost everything else in the village is older than the airfield,' Kathy pointed out. 'It was built to fulfil a temporary need, more than fifty years ago. If it's no longer needed, and obviously it isn't, then surely it makes sense to build there rather than on greenfield sites?'

'What about Hog Pond? I suppose they'll fill that in, and there's another piece of history gone. But Honeysuckle Coppice!' Charlie moaned. 'Where did they get *that* from? Why don't they call it Hog Pond Close?'

Kathy giggled. 'Oh sure. Hog Pond. A superior development of houses with unique bathing facilities.'

After lunch, Charlie settled under the shade of the apple tree with her revision. Her mother, having run out of grit for the alpine plants she was potting up, had gone to buy some from the garden centre, so when the phone rang – jangling noisily on the yard extension – Charlie answered.

'Hello, Charlie?'

It was Sean.

His familiar voice, with a trace of a Staffordshire accent, brought her first a rush of affection and then a sense of loss that was like a punch in the stomach.

'Hi, Sean! Mum's gone out. She'll only be twenty minutes.'

'No, wait.' He sounded relieved that it was Charlie

who'd picked up the phone. 'I was thinking of coming over this afternoon. Just dropping in. Do you think that would be OK?'

Charlie thought of her mother's optimistic mood today, of the success of the Nightingales visit.

'Yes, do come! She'll like that.'

'Do you think so?' Sean sounded wistful.

'Yes, I'm sure!' Charlie crossed her fingers. 'Things are going better for her lately – she's a bit more *normal.* I bet she'd like to see you.'

There was a pause, and then Sean said, 'All right, I'll come. About three-thirty?'

'Great! See you later, then.'

When Kathy arrived back, and came into the garden to ask, 'Any callers?' Charlie said, 'No,' without looking up from her Geography folder.

Sean

Charlie intended to stay out of the way, under the apple tree with her nose firmly in her revision notes, when Sean came. But it didn't work as she planned. Her mother didn't go as far as refusing to speak to Sean; it was worse than that. She treated him with distant politeness, as if he were a passing caller who might buy some of her hardy perennials. She showed him the polytunnel, the array of plants for sale, the spare stock; she showed him around the downstairs rooms of Flightsend. And then she withdrew into the old stable that she called her office, to work on her accounts. She might as well have hung a 'Do Not Disturb' notice on the door. Sean's time was up.

Charlie was the one who talked to him, who showed him the back garden and the Frühlingsmorgen rose, and who demonstrated Caspar's endearing habit of chasing after an imaginary ball and searching diligently when she pretended to throw one. It was Charlie who made Sean a cup of tea and offered to show him round the village. It was only because of

Mum that he hadn't been here before; he'd offered help with the moving in, the decorating, the setting-up of the plant nursery, but Mum had always refused.

They took Caspar. The village front gardens were drowsing in the sunshine, and collared doves cooed in the churchyard trees. A cyclist passed through with a quick burr of wheels but there was no one else in sight. Charlie thought: it could always be like this if Mum wasn't so obstinate. Sean would love living here. There was room for him at Flightsend. Theoretically.

The big ginger cat from Radbourne House was sitting on the gate-post, looking at them with calm amber eyes. Charlie said, 'I always think that cat's going to say something. It looks so intelligent. There's something about cats' eyes – well, *some* cats' eyes – that makes you think they're incredibly old and wise. Like they've been around for hundreds and hundreds of years, and seen it all.'

Rowan, if Charlie had said such a thing to her, would have stared and giggled and said, 'Charlie, you're out of your tree!' Sean laughed too, but he said, 'I know what you mean. Like Conker. He'd have talked if he could, daft old Conker. *This* cat would say something amazingly clever. He's got that sort of inscrutable look.'

Charlie thought of their old cat Conker, and the way he used to sleep on his side with his legs straight and all his paws together.

'What are you doing in the summer holidays?' she asked. 'It's only about four weeks till term ends, isn't it?' Since study leave began, she'd lost track of the dates.

'I'm going to Snowdonia for a week's mountain leadership course. Then I might go to Turkey.'

'Sounds great,' Charlie said.

'Well, I've got to do something.'

Charlie saw bleakness flicker across his face. This isn't right, she thought. Mum's done this to him. Sean had always seemed cheerful, rarely moody or depressed or even just dull; when he lived with Charlie and her mother he was always singing or whistling around the house. He'd made everything fun, even going to Tesco's – queuing at the checkout, he would organize his purchases on the cashier's belt according to some rule: by colour, or alphabetically, or in order of size. Once, recently, shopping with Mum, Charlie had found herself colour-coding the contents of their trolley as she set them out.

Sean wasn't smiling now. He'd changed in the last year; there was sadness underlying his natural vigour.

'What about you, Charlie?' he asked. 'How do you like living here? I bet you're feeling a bit cut off from Rowan and your other friends.'

'It's all right. More than all right. I like it here.'

'You're not going out with Stephen Gee any more? I don't see you around school with him, these days.'

Charlie shook her head. 'That was ages ago.'

'No one else?'

'Haven't got time,' she said lightly.

Charlie thought about asking if he'd like to go and

see the airfield, and the cross and the badger sett, but Sean said, 'I'd better go. You've got an exam tomorrow, haven't you? I don't want to stop you revising.'

'It's all right,' Charlie said, although she really *did* need to do more revision, and events seemed to be conspiring to stop her; but it was clear that Sean was really thinking about Kathy, and her offhand dismissal.

They started to walk slowly back. The Post Office-cum-shop was closed, but the front door of the cottage beside it opened as they passed, and Henrietta the shopkeeper came out holding a small watering can. She was fortyish and – Charlie thought – slightly dotty, dressing like a middle-aged hippy with strings of beads, dozens of thin bracelets that tinkled as she moved her arms, and long droopy clothes with fringes and tassels. Charlie liked her.

'Hello!' She beamed at Charlie, then at Sean; then asked Charlie, 'Is this your . . .'

There was an awkward second while Charlie imagined the words *brother? boyfriend?* hovering on Henrietta's lips. It had occurred to her before that people might think Sean was her boyfriend. She could easily pass for eighteen or nineteen if she wanted to, and Sean was still in his twenties.

'This is Sean,' Charlie said quickly. And while he smiled and said Hello back, she wondered what she *could* call him. Ex-colleague of my mother's? Mum's ex-lover? Ex-father of my mother's ex-baby?

She wished she could call him something that didn't start with *ex*.

'You won't forget about the village fête in two weeks, will you?' Henrietta said. 'I'm organizing it this year, so it's going to be fabulous.'

'No, we won't forget. Mum's having a plant stall.'

'Brilliant!' Henrietta looked Sean up and down. 'If you're around, perhaps you'd like to be in one of the tug-of-war teams? We're short of strong young men.'

'I don't think so, thanks,' Sean said.

'Oh well, never mind.' Henrietta edged past them to water the petunias in her window-boxes. Charlie knew that you shouldn't water flowers in strong sunshine, it made them wilt, but she didn't want to sound like a horticultural know-all, so said nothing. 'You ought to wear green, you know,' Henrietta told her sternly. 'It's your colour. That red T-shirt doesn't suit you at all. Far too harsh. I've got some gorgeous batik things in the shop, just arrived. Come in on Monday and have a look. Isn't green her colour?' she appealed to Sean. 'Wouldn't it look wonderful, with her hair? A sort of deep mossy green.'

'Fantastic,' Sean said.

'Bye then, Henrietta,' Charlie said firmly. When they were out of earshot – and in any case Henrietta was now singing loudly to herself as she tended her window-boxes – she said, 'Sorry about that. She's a one-off, Henrietta. You ought to see the inside of her shop. It's great – newspapers and tins of baked beans one side, joss-sticks and wind-chimes the other. I can't think who she sells her New Age stuff to. It's all green wellies and Barbour coats round here.'

'There's nothing wrong with a bit of eccentricity,' Sean said. 'And by the way, she's right about the green. You ought to get in there on Monday.'

'It's the Geography exam.'

'Give yourself a reward, then, afterwards.'

They reached the entrance to Flightsend. Sean's car was parked outside. He took his keys out of his jeans pocket and fiddled with them.

'I'm sorry if I did the wrong thing, coming,' he said. 'I just thought – oh, I don't know what.'

'I'm sorry, too,' Charlie said. 'I hoped she wouldn't be like this, not now. But well . . .'

They both looked towards the door of Kathy's office. Sean made the smallest of moves in that direction, then thought better of it. 'I won't disturb her again. Say goodbye for me.' He gave Charlie a hug, got into his car and wound down the window. He sat there for a moment, not turning the key in the ignition. Charlie thought he was about to say more.

As always, she longed to tell him: 'Come and live with us! She'll be all right. She'll come round.' But she could no longer pretend her mother was going to change her mind. Kathy was building a new life for herself, without Sean.

'I'm glad she's got you, Charleston,' Sean said. It was his nickname for her.

'I wish she had you, as well. I think she's stupid.' Charlie couldn't help saying it.

He looked down at the dashboard, not answering. Then he turned on the ignition, managed a smile, and said, 'Good luck with the exam tomorrow! I'm down to invigilate, for the first bit. I'll try not to catch your eye and put you off.'

Charlie stood outside for some minutes after the sound of his car engine had died away. Her mother didn't appear. For a moment Charlie thought of confronting her in the office, demanding to know why she'd been so rude. Then she thought of her exam, and the pathetic amount of revision she'd done so far. If she had a blazing row with Mum, she wouldn't be able to concentrate at all.

Caspar was lying flat out in the road, exhausted by his two walks and the heat. Charlie sat on the verge and thought about Sean. Since Mum had cast him off, where did that leave *her*? Sean wasn't her stepfather, he hadn't been married to Mum, and there was no name for the relationship Charlie now had with him. But that didn't mean it wasn't important to her. He was the nearest thing she had to a father; or, perhaps, father combined with elder brother.

She had disliked Sean at first, when she was only nine. She'd been suspicious of this energetic stranger who kept appearing at home, getting in the way of her and Mum. The first time Sean stayed the night, Charlie had marched into the bedroom at dawn and confronted her mother: 'Why's that man in your bed?' She'd thought he must be ill. Soon afterwards her mother had explained that Sean was coming to live with them now. Charlie's resentment had gradually faded. Sean was kind and funny, and liked inventing complicated games for her which he'd play long after Mum got tired, and by that time he was family.

I love him, she thought now, even if Mum doesn't, any more. And it was a bit difficult when someone you thought of as family turned into someone you bumped into occasionally at school.

What was wrong with Mum? Why couldn't she get back with Sean? He'd proved enough times – proved again *today* – that he still cared for her, in spite of her curtness; she was quite wrong if she'd expected him to rush off and find a younger substitute. How could she so much as look at Oliver Locke, let alone go all coy and girly about him, when there was Sean on her doorstep? Even without taking his personality into account, Charlie couldn't imagine a nicer-looking man than Sean, who was fit and tanned and had eyes of an unusual green-brown. Most women would think themselves *lucky*.

Charlie remembered a recent English lesson when Sean had been sent to cover for the absent teacher. He and her mother had only recently split up and it embarrassed her to meet him unexpectedly at school, especially like this. Shorts, polo-shirt and trainers would excite little interest on the sports field, but in the English classroom Sean's clothing – or rather his physique – drew female attention. Charlie became aware of whisperings and nudgings as he turned to write Ms Fletcher's instructions on the whiteboard. He was more interesting to the girls in the class than the relative merits of Mr Darcy and Mr Wickham in *Pride and Prejudice*. Some of the most difficult, mouthy girls, who normally sulked through lessons and spoke as rudely as they dared, instantly became charming and attentive, flicking their hair and smiling whenever Sean glanced their way.

'That's your mum's toy boy, right, Charlie?' Lisa Skillett whispered. '*Phwoarr!* Lucky her. Lucky *you*. Does she let you share?'

Charlie didn't trust herself to answer, not wanting to explain about the break-up. It wasn't the first time she'd heard Sean referred to as her mother's *toy boy*. She resented it. Just because he was younger than her mother, people assumed he wasn't to be taken seriously. And now Mum was just as bad, dumping him because she didn't think he was grown-up enough. Through some twisted logic, Mum's idea of saving Sean from sadness and loss was to hurt him even more.

Caspar, asleep, twitched his paws in the dust, probably dreaming of rabbits. Charlie picked a stem of grass and tickled his nose with it.

'Come on, Caspar. Wake up. We're going back in.'

Geography, she told herself. *Concentrate*.

She didn't see her mother until evening. Kathy stayed out in the yard and Charlie tried to revise. When she went into the kitchen to get Caspar's dinner, her mother came in. She glanced at Charlie, her expression tight and unapproachable.

'It's all right. Sean's gone,' Charlie said. She heard the hard edge to her voice.

'I didn't ask him to come.' Kathy filled the kettle and plugged it in, then looked at Charlie more closely. 'Did *you* ask him?'

'No!' Charlie spooned out the strong-smelling meat while Caspar gazed up at her. 'At least, I—'

'What?'

'He phoned while you were out,' Charlie confessed, 'and I said it would be all right to come round.'

'Really,' her mother said coldly. 'I do wish you wouldn't interfere.'

'I only thought—'

'Well, don't think. Don't interfere.'

Charlie put the bowl down on Caspar's mat. He bolted the food in great gulps, his tail waving.

'Well, what if *I* wanted to see Sean? I miss him, Mum! And at least *I* was nice to him! You were so rude – Sean was really upset, it was obvious—'

'And whose fault was that? Who told him to come round? If you'd only asked me, or told him to phone back – you must *know* I don't want him here! Anyway, I'm not having a row about it. You've got your exam tomorrow.'

'Oh yes, that's the only thing that matters!' Charlie flared. 'Typical teacher! Never mind Sean, never mind *me*! Just as long as I do well in my exam. How likely is that, now?'

They hadn't shouted at each other like this for months. All the careful adjusting Charlie had done, their frail new start, their attempts to balance on the seesaw of hope versus realism – swept away in a gush of anger. Tears of frustration prickled her eyes.

'I'm sorry,' her mother said quietly. 'I know you meant well. Let's not quarrel. If you want to see Sean, it's all right. Of course you do, and there's no reason why you shouldn't, but not *here*, OK? Now I'm going to make us something to eat. Are you hungry?'

'Yes,' said Charlie, who always was.

Later, in bed, she heard from the other room the muffled but unmistakable sound of her mother crying.

Portrait

In spite of everything, Charlie got through her Geography exam without disaster. The second History paper was on Wednesday, German on Friday, and it was all over.

Friday afternoon, after the exam, was an anticlimax. The group taking German was fairly small; most of Charlie's friends, including Rowan, had finished on Wednesday or earlier. The German candidates lingered outside for a while, adjusting to the idea of no more revision, no more sitting in silent rows, no more hand-cramp. Next Friday there would be an official leavers' day, for saying goodbye and returning books, but not everyone was coming to that. Next week, there'd be Sixth Form Induction. The word Induction, to Charlie, summoned memories of the hospital and the maternity ward. She wished they could call it something else.

It might be the last day of exams, but the bus was still leaving on time.

'Bye, then. See you at Lisa's,' Charlie called out

to two friends who'd be at the party tomorrow; then she made her way as usual to her coach.

No more exams. She slumped in her seat, trying to believe it. She felt like someone coming round from an anaesthetic.

Angus David flumped down in the seat next to hers.

'What are you doing?' she asked him.

'Balancing a beer-bottle on my nose. What's it look like?'

'You don't usually get on this bus,' Charlie explained patiently.

'Neither did you, till you moved out to the edges of the known universe. Things change.'

'Have you moved, as well?'

'No. Staying with my dad, this weekend and the next fortnight. He's the one who's moved, to Long Wykham. Sunny Long Wykham, Gateway to the Shires, famed throughout the East Midlands for its Morris dancers and sheepdog trials. Tomorrow I make my cricketing debut for the Long Wykham team, famous for its demon bowler, Andy Ferris the dairyman. Never underestimate a dairying spin-bowler.'

'I'll try not to.'

'So I'll be joining you, Charlotte of the flowing tresses.' Angus bowed, making an extravagant gesture with a twirling hand. 'I congratulate you on your unexpected luck. Feel free to bask in the glow of my sunny personality and radiant charm.'

'Well, I would if I were *coming* on the bus. I won't be,

100

apart from next Friday and the sixth form days,'
Charlie pointed out.

Angus made a clownish sad face. 'I know. Terrible
timing. Tragic. What a missed opportunity. I shall sit
here alone, dreaming of what might have been.'

'On the bus – why? Are you doing an extra exam, or
something?'

'Since you ask, my melodramatic talents are about
to be given full rein.'

'You're in the play? *A Midsummer Night's Dream?*'

'Got it in one. I'm Oberon, King of the Fairies.' He
made a camp gesture.

'Pretty solid fairy,' Charlie said, laughing. Stocky,
muscular, with hair shaved to stubble, Angus looked
like the kind of teenager people crossed the road to
avoid. Charlie knew him quite well, and that he wasn't
in the least aggressive. But King of the Fairies – well, it
would need someone with his confidence to take that
on, in front of half the school.

'Wait till you see me in my green tights.' He raised
his eyebrows suggestively. 'You won't want to miss the
theatrical event of the year, will you?'

'When is it?'

'Week after next, the same week as sixth form in-
duction. For three nights. Just wait till you see my
Titania in all her glory.' Angus made his eyes go gooey.
'How am I supposed to keep my mind on the job?'

'Who is she?'

'Pippa Woodford. Goddess of the sixth-form.
Dream-fodder for the entire male population of the

school. Pippa of the name on the walls in all the boys' bogs.'

'So that's why you wanted the part?' Charlie asked him as the bus pulled out of the gates.

'You'd think so – but no. It was just the most colossal slice of luck. I'm doing Theatre Studies next year and Ms Bishop talked me into it. That's why I'll be the only *dummkopf* from our year who's in school every day from now on. Apart from Neil Radetsky – he's Theseus.'

'D'you know your lines yet?'

'Only all the ones I say to Titania. My brain's full of obscure German vocabulary. It's an obsession, all this revision. I won't be able to stop. I won't feel happy without the periodic table in my pocket, or a list of First World War battles. At least I'll have something to read if I'm bowled out first ball.'

'You won't be,' Charlie said. 'You're one of those sickening people who's good at everything.'

'No, I'm not,' Angus said promptly. 'I'm rubbish at embroidery, for a start. And you should see me trying to do a double-axel toe-loop. Everything else, yes, OK.'

'Idiot,' Charlie said, pretending to hit him. 'Why are you always so *energetic*? Most people are wiped out after weeks of exams, but here you are – bounding about like those dogs in adverts. Do you take Bob Martin's or something?'

'Every day, with my Pedigree Chum,' Angus said. 'I'll roll over for you to tickle my tummy, if you like.

Fancy coming to the cricket tomorrow? We need a few tame females to brew up the tea and do the washing-up.'

'*Tame females* – well, look elsewhere. What century do you think this is? Are male cricketers incapable of making tea?' Charlie retorted. 'So you're not going to Lisa's party, then? Cricket takes up the entire evening when you include the ball-by-ball dissection in the pub afterwards.' She knew because Sean had sometimes played.

'That's right. Can't miss the post-mortem. Lisa's party will have to manage without me.'

Soon after Charlie got home, Rowan phoned.

'You're still OK for tomorrow night? We'll come round and pick you up, about half-eight.'

'We?'

'Russell, me and Fraser. I *told* you.'

'Fraser can give me a lift home, you said. You didn't say he was *taking* me there. I've asked Mum.'

'Save her the trouble, can't you? What's the problem?'

Charlie was having misgivings about the party, and going with Fraser. She'd forgotten to ask Fay for the evening off, but now realized that she needn't; if the others weren't coming till half-past eight, she could do her waitressing first, and leave a bit early.

'Pick me up at Nightingales, could you?' she asked Rowan. 'Not here. It's the big house round the bend, with the high stone wall.'

'You're going there first? But when will you get

ready?' For Rowan, getting ready for a party took up most of the afternoon.

'Five minutes in the staff loo, that's all I need.'

'Charlie, are you kidding?'

Rowan sounded as if she thought Fraser would be getting a poor deal.

Charlie reported for Friday-night duty. 'What have we got this weekend, then?' she asked Suzanne, as they set the table.

'Your art chap again,' Suzanne said, 'and Yoga meditation. Spot the Yogi.'

'They're going to spend the whole weekend meditating?'

'I might join them,' Suzanne said. 'Jason was ill during the night and I was up three times. I could pretend to meditate but really be fast asleep.'

Charlie saw Oliver Locke in the entrance hall when she went to clear wine glasses. The hall was full of the usual polite chit-chat, *Have you just arrived?* and *What a beautiful spot.* Oliver, in the middle of it, caught Charlie's eye with what looked like relief, and raised his glass.

'Exams all over! Feeling de-mob happy?' He came over to her.

'No, more like numb,' Charlie said. 'It'll take a while to get used to it. What's your course this time?'

'Portraiture. I told you. Do you want to join us tomorrow?'

'I might,' Charlie said. She had enjoyed painting

the self-portrait for her coursework. 'If you're sure I won't be in the way—'

'Fay!' Oliver signalled across the room, and Fay broke off her conversation and came over. 'It's all right if Charlie joins my group, isn't it? There's space for one more, no problem.'

'Of course. Oh, you two know each other from school?' Fay was wearing one of her elegant dresses; when there were no visitors around, she wore jeans and a shirt, like Charlie's mother.

Charlie took advantage of the meeting by saying, 'Would it be OK if I left a bit early tomorrow night, after we've served the coffee? Suzanne and Jon don't mind. I can make up the time on Sunday.'

'Saturday night gadding?' Oliver asked, with a lift of his eyebrows.

'Lisa Skillet's having a party to celebrate the end of the exams.'

'Yes, that's fine,' Fay said. 'I was meaning to ask if you could do some child-minding for me, now you've got more time. I thought you might like the extra money. It'd be the odd couple of hours here and there, maybe twice a week. Rosie's not really much trouble.'

'Yes, OK.'

'Could you do Tuesday afternoon, two till four? I've got a meeting with one of our sponsors.'

Why, Charlie asked herself afterwards, why did I say yes? How am I going to tell Mum?

She thought of spending time with Rosie, who was

only a little older than their own Rose would have been. Rosie always made Charlie think of her lost sister, and yet she was surprised to find that she *did* want to do it. Wanted to see if she could. Was it like licking a sore tooth? she wondered. Or a more positive step forward – stop pretending that two-year-old children didn't exist?

She told her mother later that evening: first about the portraiture class, and then, casually, about the child-minding. All Kathy said was, 'Well, Charlie, we needn't have worried about you being bored, living here. With the waitressing, and walking Caspar, and the art class and now this –' Charlie noted the phrasing, the avoidance of words like *Rosie* or *baby-sitting* – 'there's not much time for sitting about twiddling your thumbs.'

Charlie was irritated by the phrase *twiddling your thumbs.* It wasn't the sort of thing her mother would usually say; and Charlie was annoyed by the implication that she was dull enough to sit about with nothing to do. There was a coolness between them, since the weekend.

In the morning she took her drawing things to Nightingales with her, as well as jeans and a shirt to change into after her breakfast stint. Oliver Locke's class was held in the Long Barn, an outhouse converted into a studio. It was a large, airy building with windows set into the roof, its agricultural origins shown by the hayloft doors above the entrance and the pitchforks, scythes and other tools mounted on the walls.

Charlie arrived late after clearing up in the kitchen. The other course members – some fifteen of them – were already seated at their easels, around a female model who sat in an upright chair, reading a book. Oliver Locke came over to Charlie, and showed her to an easel.

'This is Charlie, everyone,' he announced. 'You've seen her in waitressing garb. She'll be joining us.'

The others looked at her and smiled, and one or two said Hello. As usual, most were middle-aged or over; Charlie was by far the youngest person in the room. The model was a woman of about forty, wearing glasses, which Charlie thought would be difficult to draw.

She settled at the easel, then set up her sketchpad, took out her 2B pencils and her putty rubber. The atmosphere was silent and serious, everyone concentrating hard. Oliver moved around looking at the drawings, sometimes making a low-voiced comment, sometimes just watching. After a while he sat down and worked on a drawing of his own.

Charlie sketched, rubbed out, frowned, turned a page and started again. She was looking at the model from rather a difficult angle, from the front and slightly to one side, and the woman's face was foreshortened, tilted down at her book. She drew in the eyebrows and forehead and then went hopelessly wrong with the angle of the glasses. No one else seemed to be having problems; she could see the drawing of the person nearest her, already well into the sheen on the model's hair and the moulding of her lips. And yet, last week, Oliver had told Charlie that she had more talent than anyone on the course. They must have been a particularly hopeless lot, she thought now.

Discouraged, she looked across to where he sat at his easel. He was sitting to the left of the model, drawing quickly. I'd rather draw him, she thought. His pose was attractive: sitting forward in his seat, his face in profile, concentrated. There was a gracefulness about his movements and she knew she could draw the folds in his shirt and the way the light defined his shoulders. She felt it in her fingers, the urge to work, to commit what she saw to paper. She turned a page and began sketching rapidly: not a portrait but the whole figure. This was easier, much more satisfying. The proportions came out just right, as she knew they would; she had caught the pose.

Then Oliver stood up and went to the person nearest him, making a comment. Charlie went back to her inadequate portrait and tried to sketch in the glasses, her obstacle. Doubt was making her pencil strokes hesitant. She was muffling, and she knew that was no way to draw.

'You're having trouble getting started, aren't you?' Oliver spoke close behind her. 'It's an awkward angle you've got. I haven't helped you much by sitting you here.'

'It's the glasses,' Charlie explained.

She was disappointed that he'd seen how useless she was.

'Here, let me show you.' For a second his hand curved over hers. He took the pencil, and before she realized it he'd turned the page and was looking at the drawing of himself.

'Oh, I – got side-tracked.' Charlie felt a rush of heat to her face.

But Oliver only laughed, and studied the drawing carefully. 'Now *that's* better. That's more like your real work. It's got all the freedom and confidence that's lacking so far in the portrait. Here, try it like this.' In a corner of the sheet, he deftly sketched in the model's forehead, the eyebrows, the glasses. 'Look at the way the glasses rest on the bridge of the nose. The way the sides of the glasses come out beyond the brow-bone. The angle of the lenses. That's what you're not getting yet.'

He moved on, and Charlie tried again, finding it easier. Listening to him talk about *the brow-bone, the nose*, she felt less embarrassed about the impromptu sketch. To an art teacher, bodies and faces were just objects occupying space, shapes with curves and planes and textures. She worked more steadily now. Next time he came to look, he just nodded approvingly and went on. After a while there was a break for the model, and do-it-yourself coffee made from an urn on the trestle table. People looked at each other's drawings, and one of the women complimented Charlie on hers.

'Oh, you're *good*. Are you an art student?'

Charlie had thought she might go home at lunchtime, but Oliver clearly expected her to stay all day. When they broke for lunch – just sandwiches and fruit laid out buffet-style in the dining-room – he told her, 'I've brought a book for you. Philip Wilson Steer. Come over to the Well House with me on the way back and I'll get it for you.'

The Well House was a tiny cottage, close to the Long Barn, usually used for accommodation for one of the tutors; the other had a small flat above the stables. Charlie was curious about the Well House, which was tiny and octagonal, like a garden summerhouse. If there'd ever been a well, there wasn't one now.

'I like it here,' Oliver said, as they walked down the narrow path. 'It's well away from everyone. I always ask for the Well House.'

'Why don't you go home at night?' Charlie asked. 'You must live fairly close?' She wondered if he were married, or living with someone.

Oliver pulled a key out of his pocket and unlocked the green front door. 'It's only temporary, where I'm living. I'm in the middle of what you might call an upheaval. That's why I'm here so much just now. Fay and Dan are good friends, and I like helping them out.'

'Are you married?' Charlie asked.

He looked at her. 'Not any more.'

He stood back for her to go in first. She was disconcerted to find herself in his bedroom; not that she shouldn't have known, as it was obvious from the outside that the Well House had only one main room. There was a bed, a desk, flowered curtains at the window, a bookshelf laden with art books. The bed was neatly made, and a pair of his boots stood at the foot. Through a door she could see into a tiny tiled bathroom. Oliver followed her in, leaving the front door open.

'Here it is.' He pulled down a glossy book from the shelf. 'Philip Wilson, your namesake. You can borrow it. Keep it as long as you like.'

She flicked it open, and saw inside the front cover: *To Oliver, with love from Rosalind.*

'My ex-wife.' He saw her reading it.

'Is she an artist?'

'No. She's a librarian.'

Charlie wondered about the break-up. Was there another story here of loss, loneliness and rejection? Was Rosalind obstinate and unapproachable, like Mum? She longed to know more, but felt that she'd been blunt enough already.

Oliver looked at his watch. 'Come on. It's time to get back.'

Saturday Night

Charlie had had enough of this party. It was nearly one in the morning and she'd have to be up again in six hours' time. Rowan and Russell had disappeared into one of the bedrooms, and she didn't want to be the one to disturb them. Fraser Goff, supposedly keen for her to come, had said little to her all evening and was now wrapped round Lisa's friend Dawn who was wearing what looked like a black nightdress. Charlie's ex-boyfriend, Stephen Gee, had made a big show of arriving with a glamorous dark girl called Melinda from a different school, and kept looking at Charlie to make sure she'd seen. Charlie hadn't taken much notice of any of this earlier in the evening, when she'd been laughing and joking with a group who were looking at Lisa's photos of last year's ski trip, but by now the party had deteriorated. A second wave – friends of Lisa's older brother – had arrived after the pub closed, and colonized the kitchen. There was so much dope in the garden that a sweet-smelling drift came in whenever anyone opened the door, and head-thumping music made conversation impossible. Lisa's parents had gone away for the weekend, leaving Lisa and her brother, Rob, to clear up next day, so there was no reason for the party to end this side of Sunday afternoon. Charlie had fended off a drunken friend of Rob's who lurched at her in a waft of beer and sweat, and now she wanted to go home.

'Hey, you know who's not here, Lisa?' she heard Dawn saying. 'Aberdeen Angus!'

'Oh, Angus is a prat,' Fraser said. 'He'll be rehearsing for the play. You know he's King of the Fairies? I mean, who else would volunteer for that?'

'In green tights!' There were shrieks of laughter.

'Let's all go! Get front row seats!'

Charlie couldn't help sticking up for Angus. 'I think it's brave of him. Not many people would have the nerve.'

'Not many people would have the *legs*.'

'Not many people would have the utter stupidity,' Lisa said. 'I mean, imagine hauling yourself into school every day, after everyone else has left.'

'So, are you disappointed he didn't come tonight, Charlie?' Dawn asked, in a snidey way.

'Oh yeah, Angus for Charlie!' Fraser made smooching noises. 'Woah! They're an item – latest celebrity couple! Call *Hello!* magazine!'

Rowan must have made it up, about him wanting me to come tonight, Charlie thought. She looked at her watch and considered phoning her mother.

'Don't get a lift home from anyone who's had too much to drink,' Kathy had told her. 'I'd rather come and fetch you myself. I don't like the idea of you being driven about by someone I don't know. Someone *you* hardly know, by the sound of it.'

Charlie knew that her mother would be lying awake, waiting for her to come in. Kathy never complained about it – she trusted Charlie not to do anything daft – but was unable to sleep until she was safely indoors. When Charlie thought of all the disasters that could possibly befall her – car accidents, kidnap, murder, death from sudden illness – she worried more on her mother's account than on her own. She couldn't let Kathy down by getting herself killed, maimed or disfigured. Kathy would never get over it.

All the same, Charlie didn't want to drag her out of bed at this hour, if Fraser could take her. He was being loud and unfunny, but she didn't think he'd drunk too much. She looked across at Lisa, who was sitting in a very drawable, languid pose, sprawled on the sofa with one leg curled underneath her and an arm draped over the cushioned back. Charlie thought of the drawing she could do if only she had a sketchbook and pencil; thought of showing it to Oliver Locke tomorrow.

She'd had enough of sitting about. She went to find Rowan, and found her coming downstairs trailing Russell by the hand.

'Where've you been? I want to go home,' Charlie said.

'We were just coming to look for you.' Rowan giggled. 'We fell asleep.'

'Oh, is *that* what you've been doing?' Charlie asked, sceptically. 'Let's collect Fraser, then, and go. If we can prise him away from Dawn.'

Dawn, hearing about the arrangements, said she was coming, too. Charlie was relieved to find that they were all coming out to Lower Radbourne in the car, rather than Fraser dropping them off at their much nearer homes before taking her on alone.

They got into Fraser's battered Escort, Dawn in the passenger seat, Charlie in the back with Russell and Rowan. Fraser put a CD in the stereo and turned up the volume. He drove far more aggressively than he had on the way to the party.

'Careful, there'll be police about,' Dawn warned. 'Lisa's brother got nicked last Saturday, speeding.'

Fraser slowed, but once out of town on the country lanes he put his foot down again. He and Dawn were singing along to the music, something Charlie didn't recognize; Russell had fallen asleep against Rowan's shoulder.

Charlie closed her eyes, thinking of Flightsend and bed; then she opened them wide as the car leapt away from a junction. Fraser was driving with one hand on the wheel, his spare arm round Dawn's neck, and Dawn was giggling and leaning against him. Knowing the lanes well, Charlie kept her gaze fixed on the road ahead, the hedges and gateways illuminated by the headlights. She needed to provide a more attentive pair of eyes for Fraser.

'Fraser, slow down – *slow down!* – there's a sharp bend here—' she called out.

They were approaching the corner by Devil's Spinney, a right-angled bend. Fraser braked, not enough. He jerked his spare arm from behind Dawn and grabbed the wheel, losing control so that Charlie saw tree trunks looming dizzily in front of them.

'Oh! Look out!' Dawn shrieked. 'There's a dog, or something—'

Fraser wrenched at the wheel. Charlie felt a small thud of impact, and Dawn screamed as the front of the car tilted and came to a stop, centimetres away from a gatepost. Fraser clicked off the stereo. Charlie's ears buzzed in the sudden, blessed silence. It felt like being on a roller-coaster that had come to an abrupt stop, her insides swinging back to their normal place.

'What?' Russell asked blearily.

Dawn clapped both hands over her face. 'Oh, you hit it – that dog!'

Caspar. The image of Caspar dead and bleeding by the roadside leapt into Charlie's brain, though there was no reason why he'd be wandering the lanes on his own at night. Her hands shook as she fumbled with the door catch. She felt drunk and befuddled, although she hadn't had much to drink. She didn't want to see, but she had to.

Dawn had got out too, stumbling in her high heels. 'Uurgh! Don't *touch* it! Oh, gross!'

It was a fox, hit a glancing blow and thrown into the middle of the road. There was enough moonlight for Charlie to see the gleam of teeth, the pale fur under the chin, the bushy tail. A cub, she thought. She touched it carefully, feeling the warmth, the softness of the fur. She had heard and felt the impact; a young creature couldn't survive that.

She turned on Fraser, who was examining the front of his car. 'Look what you've done!'

'It's not my bloody fault!' he retaliated. 'The thing was just *there*.'

'Oh no, what shall we do?' Dawn wailed. She stood shivering, huddling herself in her arms.

'If you back the car off the verge, I'll see better in the headlights,' Charlie told Fraser.

'Sod that. What is it, a fox? You see dozens of the things dead on the roads.'

Dawn started to cry. 'Oh, the poor little thing. Is it dead, Charlie?'

'What's happened?' Rowan came over to look. 'Did we kill it? Oh no, how awful! Is it all bloody?'

'I don't know. I'm not leaving it here, in the middle of the road,' Charlie said.

'Uurgh! You're not going to *touch* it!' Dawn jumped back and clung to Fraser.

Charlie lifted the limp weight of the fox cub and carried it round to the front of the car. In the beam of the headlights she could see its eyes glazing in death, its mouth parted. She didn't want to look more closely in case there was some horrible injury.

'What *is* it?' Rowan asked.

'A fox cub. A beautiful fox cub.' Charlie carried it through the gateway and laid it down gently in the long grass under a tree. She thought: if I hadn't agreed to this, it'd still be alive.

'Ugh, Charlie! You'll catch fleas.' Dawn was half-giggling, half-crying, leaning against Fraser. 'Is it dead?'

'Did you hit a tree?' Russell asked Fraser, fully awake now.

'No, only just missed it. I swerved to avoid that damn thing. The car's all right.'

'You were going too fast,' Charlie said. 'Much too fast.'

Fraser glared at her. 'Don't start treating me like a murderer. It's only a fox, for Christ's sake. There are dozens of the things wandering about the roads. What did you expect me to do, crash the car? Kill us all?'

'You were already out of control, before the fox!' Charlie flashed. 'If you hadn't been driving so fast—'

'Well, I was! What are you, Special Branch or something? Going to report me for dangerous driving?'

'Oh, do stop *arguing*,' Dawn said, sniffing. 'It's dead now. Hadn't you better move the car, Fraser, in case something comes round the bend?'

They all stood aside while Fraser started the engine and reversed off the verge. Dawn, Russell and Rowan got back in, and Charlie saw Rowan fastening her seat belt; she hadn't bothered before.

'Get in, Charlie,' Fraser said curtly through the driver's window.

'No thanks. I'll walk.'

'Don't be an idiot. Get in.'

'*Don't* tell me what to do!'

'Oh, but *Charlie*,' Dawn wailed. 'You can't walk off on your own in the middle of the night, miles from anywhere!'

'I'm not miles from anywhere. I'm nearly home.'

Charlie reached into the car for the small rucksack she'd taken to the party, with her keys in it; then she said a curt 'Bye,' and turned to walk the half-mile back to the village. She breathed the cool night air, reassured by the safe, familiar sounds of her footsteps on tarmac and leaves overhead stirring in a faint breeze. An owl screeched somewhere nearby. The car stayed where it was for a few moments; then, presumably urged by Dawn or Rowan, Fraser drove slowly behind her, all the way home, in a ridiculous procession. She didn't look back. When she got to Flightsend, Fraser reversed down the track, yelled at her, 'Don't bother saying thanks for the lift, or anything!' and pulled away fast, with a squeal of tyres.

Charlie let herself in, and was greeted by a sleepy Caspar. Kathy came to the top of the stairs in her nightshirt, and called down: 'Who was that shouting? How was the party?'

'Awful. Really awful,' Charlie said. She'd been longing for bed but was now wide awake, and furious. 'I'll tell you in a minute. D'you want coffee?'

There was a different model for Sunday's portrait class – an old man, with a craggy, interesting face. No glasses this time, but lots of wrinkles. By the coffee break, Charlie had produced two sketches, one of which she intended to work up during the afternoon. She'd miss part of the next session, as she was due in the kitchen an hour before lunch, which was always a traditional roast on Sundays.

Everyone took their coffee out to the lawn. Charlie, seeking shade, found a place under the mulberry tree, and Oliver Locke came to join her.

'How was the party?'

'Terrible.' Charlie wasn't going to explain; she wanted to forget about it.

'Why? Boyfriend stand you up?'

Charlie shook her head. 'I haven't got a boyfriend.' And didn't particularly want one, she'd realized at the party; there was no one there she was remotely interested in. She liked some of the boys from her form, but only as friends. They were all so *immature*, she thought now. Especially Fraser Goff, who was a year older.

'How well do you know Sean?' she asked Oliver.

'Sean?' He was lying back on the grass, looking up at the canopy of leaves.

'Sean Freeland, PE teacher.'

'Oh, *that* Sean. Seems a nice guy. He's one of those muscular, athletic types that makes the rest of us feel flabby and wimpish. I don't know him at all well, no.

Why d'you ask? Are you going to tell me you're hopelessly in love with him? At least two of the girls in my form are.'

'No! I just wondered. So you don't know about him and—'

Oliver lifted his head. 'No, who?'

'Him and my mum.'

Charlie wished she hadn't started this; she'd assumed he would know about Sean and her mother. But there were sixty-something people on the staff, and Sean, being a PE teacher, was busy most lunchtimes with practices and matches. Oliver's department was in a separate building, and the art teachers were a close-knit group. It wasn't really surprising if he and Sean hardly knew each other.

'Sean Freeland and your mum?' He raised himself on his elbows to look at her. 'Are they going out?'

'Not any more. Sean lived with us for five years.'

'When your mum was on the staff? I remember her, vaguely, the year I started. She left to have a baby, didn't she? Why did they split up?'

Oh God. She'd have to tell him the whole story.

Then she saw, to her vast relief, the plump woman called Audrey – the one who'd complimented her on her drawing yesterday – coming over the grass towards them.

'Charlie,' she called out, 'you live in the village, don't you? Do you know the local footpaths? Sheila and I were thinking of going for a walk later, before we go home.'

'Sure, there's a map in the entrance hall.' Charlie got quickly to her feet. 'I'll show you.'

Rowan phoned that evening. 'I'm sorry about last night. I've tried to phone you three times already. It wasn't a very good party, was it?'

'I'm surprised you noticed,' Charlie said.

Rowan ignored this. 'And I'm sorry about Fraser. I mean, he *told* Russell he liked you, he really did. I know you must think I was making it up, but I wasn't, honestly.'

'You think I'm *disappointed*? I couldn't care less about Fraser. He's a total nerd who killed a fox and was more bothered about his stupid car.'

'It was awful about the fox. Dawn cried nearly all the way home.'

'*Dawn!*' Charlie said scornfully. 'Fraser's welcome to her.'

'I hope you don't think it was my fault,' Rowan said. 'Because I really did want you to have a good time. There's this other party next Saturday—'

'No thanks. I'll be working.'

'Well, when will I see you? We're going to Tenerife for a fortnight, the Monday after the sixth form days. D'you want to come over before we go?'

She could offer to come here, Charlie thought. She said, 'I'm a bit busy at the moment.'

'What with?' Rowan sounded curious. 'Have you met someone, out there in the sticks?'

To Rowan, *meeting someone* meant meeting a boy.

'Of course I haven't,' Charlie said. 'Who is there to meet? I'll see you at the leavers' do on Friday. Are you going to the play? *A Midsummer Night's Dream*? I am, if I can get time off.'

Rowan giggled. 'Aberdeen Angus in his fairy costume? Oh yes, I'm not missing that.'

Charlie rang off, thinking without real envy of Rowan's Tenerife trip. Rowan's family always had a beach holiday, never venturing far from their chosen resort, bringing back photos of themselves by the poolside which might as well have been taken in their back garden. Russell was going with them this time; otherwise Rowan would probably have refused to go.

Charlie and her mother didn't have money to spare for going away, and anyway Kathy couldn't leave her nursery plants at this time of year. Charlie's last holiday had been five days with her mother and grandmother in Scarborough last summer. Before that, there had been trips to the Lake District with Sean and Mum, staying in a cottage. Charlie thought of boat trips on Coniston Water, walks on the fells, huge meals afterwards in Ambleside or Keswick: the only kind of holiday she knew. She thought of the names of the fells – wonderful, evocative names. Helvellyn and Haystacks. Cat Bells, Red Screes and Blencathra.

Moving into her bedroom at Flightsend, sorting through her stuff, Charlie had found an old photograph of herself and Sean on the summit of Great Gable, taken by Mum. They were both smiling and windblown, Sean in a green fleece, Charlie twelve and unselfconscious, with her hair in plaits. She remembered that day: the long, hot ascent, the worn scree paths near the summit, herself and Mum tiring, Sean encouraging, then the triumph of reaching the top, and not wanting to go down. Charlie liked that photo, and the memories that went with it, and had pinned it to her cork board. Her mother, in and out of the bedroom, must have noticed it there but had never once referred to it. It might have been three strangers who climbed Great Gable.

Landing

Charlie laid out the portraits on the kitchen table to show Kathy, who was impressed.

'They're *very* good. Especially that one.' She pointed to the portrait of the old man. 'I mean, I've never seen that man but I feel as if I have. He looks as if he's about to open his mouth and speak to me.'

'Yes, I like that one best. Mr Locke – Oliver – is a brilliant teacher. He can always tell you just the right thing when you're stuck.'

'I think the whole Art department is very strong, judging by the results,' her mother said. 'What's the name of that young woman, the head of department? Oh – Lizzie something – Lizzie Pearson. She's supposed to be outstandingly good. And there's that older man, Nigel something, who's had screen-prints exhibited at the Arts Centre.'

Charlie felt unreasonably annoyed by the implication that anyone could be as good as Oliver Locke. Anyway, she hadn't been talking about school. There would be a two-week gap before Oliver next came to Nightingales – next weekend's courses were Butterflies and Moths of Northamptonshire, and Map-Reading for Beginners. She was determined to have something good to show him in a fortnight's time, something she would do on her own. She thought she might do some drawing on the airfield, try to capture its atmosphere of isolation.

Kathy had completed her garden plans for Nightingales and was due to show them to Dan and Fay that afternoon, while Charlie looked after the plant shop. The plans, drawn to scale on squared paper, with a separate plant-list, looked very professional to Charlie, but her mother was anxious. 'I've never done this before – worked properly to scale, or planned in such detail. With my own garden, it's all instinct and guesswork.'

'You should think about it,' Charlie told her. 'Offering a garden design service. You could put an ad in the paper. It's the trendy thing nowadays, isn't it – having someone design your garden?'

'Who'd take me on? I haven't got any qualifications.'

'You could *get* some.' Charlie, who occasionally browsed through her mother's gardening magazines, had seen short design courses on offer, with diplomas awarded at the end. 'It doesn't really matter what. Just as long as you get letters after your name.'

'I've already got letters,' her mother reminded her. 'BA. And PGCE. Post-Graduate Certificate in

Education,' she added in response to Charlie's puzzled look.

'Well, you can use those. Pretend it stands for – wait – Botanical Adviser. Professor of Garden Creativity Extraordinaire.'

Kathy looked sceptical. 'Hmm. Are you taking Caspar out?'

'Yes. Now.' Charlie cleared away her drawings.

She thought she might draw the rusted cross and the long grasses at the foot of the tree, but although she walked confidently to what she thought was the place, she couldn't find it. She couldn't see the cross, or the badger sett. Caspar was no help, more interested in snapping at the brown butterflies that fluttered among the grasses. It couldn't be *that* difficult; all she had to do was follow the perimeter fence. The hot, dry weather had turned the colours all tawny: bleached grasses, rust-coloured sorrel, yellow hawkbit.

It was a hazy day, the air still and the sun muted behind a thin cloud layer. Intent on pushing her way through the brambles that clung to her jeans and meshed her feet, she didn't notice the sound of the aircraft until it had become a persistent drone. She looked up, squinting into the brightness. Her heart thumped. It was like the first time: the small aircraft coming out of the haze, slowly but perceptibly descending over the field. Charlie stood rooted to the spot, staring. She wasn't exposed on the runway as before; she felt no urge to dive for cover, more the sense of being in a dream, of watching something that had happened before, and seemed inevitable. The engine noise, now a throaty roar, filled her senses.

'Caspar! Caspar!' She wanted him with her. He'd heard the aircraft engine too, and was facing it like a pointer, ears and tail alert. The little plane circled overhead, and then the pilot aligned it with the main runway. It was coming in to land.

It must be in trouble, surely! There was no control tower here, no windsock, and the runway was hardly fit to land on. Charlie's stomach lurched: what would she do if it crashed in front of her? What if it burst into flames? There was no one to help. The plane came down slowly, looking as frail as a leaf riding the wind; it wavered, levelled, touched down. She heard the screech of wheels on uneven tarmac, and the aircraft seemed to leap forward, racing along the runway. She gripped Caspar's collar, expecting the plane to rush on out of control, to crash in the thick hawthorn hedge at the end.

The pilot brought it to a halt. She saw the blur of propellers, and then the engine was turned off and they whirred into stillness. She could read the plane's registration letters, see that it was bigger and more substantial than she'd imagined. With the drama over – no crash, no spurt of flame, no horribly injured victims requiring help – Charlie hesitated, still holding Caspar. A door at the side of the cockpit slid open and the pilot, a slim man, jumped down. Half expecting a Biggles-like figure, Charlie was surprised to see that he wasn't wearing flying overalls or goggles, just ordinary black trousers and sweater. She had the odd sense of switching from one kind of film – aircraft disaster – to other scenarios all mixed together. Her thoughts raced. Foiled terrorist? Transworld flier makes landfall? Ghost plane returns from World War Two mission? Or even – teenage girl abducted from airfield?

She was near enough to the stile and the footpath into Hog's Pond field to make a run for it if she wanted, but curiosity made her stand and watch. The pilot crouched, and touched the runway with both hands – almost caressed it. Charlie had seen this done by Popes, presidents and returning hostages – a symbolic gesture, but here there were no journalists or camera crews to record its significance. Just the pilot, not knowing he was watched.

Then he stood up and walked straight towards her.

Caspar gave two sharp barks, and she heard the growl in his throat. The man stopped, stared, as if seeing Charlie and Caspar for the first time. Then he raised a hand, signalling that he was friendly.

'All right, Caspar,' Charlie said, putting her hand on his head. He was still tensed, watching the man closely. For the first time Charlie thought he might make a good guard dog. No one would attack her while she had Caspar. She hoped.

She could see now that the man was much older than she'd thought at first – fiftyish, she thought. He had the slim build of a younger man but his hair was greying and his face lined.

'I'm very sorry if I startled you,' he said. He came forward and stopped, not too close. 'I didn't expect anyone to be here.' He spoke in an accent Charlie couldn't instantly place.

Her nervousness released itself in a laugh that came out too loudly. 'I didn't expect a plane to land here. I didn't know the airfield was in use.'

The man gave a thin smile. 'Officially it is not. You were here the other day, I think? With your dog?'

'I saw you flying over. Low over the runway. Then you flew on. I thought you were lost.'

'No, I was not lost.'

She recognized his accent now. German. She realized it with an illogical tingling of fear, thinking of the place's wartime origins. She thought: I'm here, alone, talking to a strange German pilot. On this airfield where British pilots trained to bomb German cities. Cologne, Hamburg, Dresden. Her mind flashed up images of smoking rubble, of people throwing themselves into the river Elbe to escape the flames. She'd answered a question on Bomber Command policy in her History exam last week. The crazy idea came to her that this German pilot had come back for revenge.

'Is it your own plane, then?' she asked. 'You came here on purpose? All the way from . . . from . . .'

'From Leicester. I have flown here from a flying club in Leicester, where I live. Yes, it is my own aircraft, the

130

Cessna.' Then he smiled. 'Oh, I see. You think from my accent that I have flown all the way from Germany, yes?'

Charlie nodded.

'I have not lived in Germany for many years,' the man told her. 'Since a student. For a while I live here in this village.'

Charlie was confused by the tense. *Used* to live? Or *am* living?

'And you?' the man went on. 'You live nearby?'

'In the village.' Charlie pointed. 'Lower Radbourne. I often walk here. Why have you—'

'Why have I landed here? I am searching for something.'

He hesitated, looking at her. Then he bent down to Caspar, holding out a hand to be sniffed. Caspar's demeanour changed instantly from suspicion to pleasure; he wriggled, licking the man's hand. For the first time, Charlie thought: I needn't be afraid. He's a man who likes dogs and knows how to treat them.

'Looking for—?' she prompted.

'Yes.' The man straightened. 'Looking for a cross. When I lived in the village I used to walk on the air-field as you do. The cross was here then.'

'The cross! That's what *I* was looking for!'

He stared. 'You have seen it?'

'Yes, last week! It's—'

Charlie remembered that she'd been unable to find it just now. She turned to point at the perimeter fence,

131

and found that she was looking straight at the ash tree that had eluded her before. That, she realized, was where he'd been aiming, before he saw her.

'It's here,' she said. 'I found it by accident. Well, Caspar did, really.'

'Your dog?'

He was already walking towards the tree. He knelt on the ground by the cross, and stretched out a hand.

'Still there. I am always afraid it will be taken. Thrown away as rubbish.'

'What's it for?' Charlie asked. 'I wondered.'

'It's a memorial to my father,' he said, not looking at her. 'He died here, in 1943.'

'In the war.' She was looking down at his neat parting, his dark hair with silver in it. Surely he couldn't be old enough to remember the war.

'Yes. My father was a Luftwaffe pilot. He flew a Junkers 88. In March 1943 he crash-landed here and was killed. The landing gear of the Junkers was damaged – it was impossible to make a proper landing. The two other members of his crew baled out, but my father did not. The aircraft burst into flames.'

He stated all this matter-of-factly, kneeling with one hand on the cross.

'How old were you?' Charlie asked.

'I was not yet born at that time. I was born two months later, in Hamburg.'

Charlie imagined a woman, seven months pregnant, opening her door to receive the telegram she must have dreaded.

'So,' said the man, 'I know my father only by my mother's memories, and his photographs.'

'That's like me,' Charlie told him. 'I never knew my father, either.'

'Your father was killed?'

'No. He left. When I was two he left us and went back to Canada. I can't remember him. I know what he looked like, from his photo. That's all.'

'That is very sad,' the man said. He touched the cross again, with both hands, then stood up and brushed dried earth from the knees of his trousers. Now that he'd seen the cross, Charlie wondered if he'd climb into his plane and fly away. She'd listened to his story with a sense of confirmation rather than surprise: I knew, she thought, I *knew* something had happened here. She had the odd notion that her discovery of the cross, her wondering, had summoned him out of the skies. When he took off again, he and his plane would be as insubstantial as thistledown, as a dream. Perhaps she *was* dreaming. But she looked at the man and saw the stitching around the crew neck of his sweater and the check fabric of a shirt underneath. Undreamlike details. His appearance was very neat: grey-streaked hair, well-ironed trousers, black boots, tanned hands, clean fingernails.

'Who put the cross here?' she asked. 'Did you?'

'No, I believe the cross was given by the English airmen, the RAF staff who were based here. A tribute to an enemy pilot who faced the same dangers they did.'

'How do you know that?'

'From the survivors, the ones who baled out. They were captured, held as prisoners-of-war. But afterwards, when the war was over, they came here to make their farewells to my father, and they found the cross. They told this to my mother.'

'So you came to find it.'

'Yes. When I came to study in Cambridge I made my way to your village, to this airfield. The place has haunted me ever since.' He said it unselfconsciously, as if stating a simple fact. 'After Cambridge I work for many years in Nottingham, but I visited here many times. By car, then,' he added, gesturing towards the aircraft. 'It is only later that I learn to fly, and get my pilot's licence. And gradually I fell in love with this village. You live here, you say, in Lower Radbourne? Do you live in one of the old village houses, or perhaps a modern one?'

'Ours is an old house, a cottage,' Charlie told him. 'It's called Flightsend.'

'You live at Flightsend,' the pilot said slowly, gazing at her. 'How very strange then that I should meet you here.'

Charlie stared at him.

'Flightsend was my home,' he said. 'It is I who named it Flightsend. Before, it was Glebe Cottage. I'm glad it still has the name I gave it.'

'You lived in our house?'

'Yes, it was my home until six years ago. Is it much changed?' the man asked wistfully.

'Hardly at all, I should think. Apart from my mum's

134

polytunnel, for her plants. She's a gardener, she runs a nursery. Why don't you come home now, and see? My mother would love to meet you, to hear all about— She's a History teacher – I mean used to be. She knows a lot about, about the war.'

'I would love to,' the man said. 'But I can't leave the aircraft here. It is unauthorized landing, you see. I have no permission to be here. I am a trespasser.'

Charlie was reluctant to give up her idea. 'You could hide it,' she suggested. 'Park it –' she wasn't sure if *park* was the right word to use for an aircraft – 'over there, close to the trees. Then unless the farmer actually comes over here, he won't know.'

She could tell that he really wanted to see Flightsend. He smiled and said. 'All right. I'll take the risk.' Then, formally, he held out his right hand. 'My name is Dietmar Kolbert. And yours?'

Walking with Dietmar down the lane, Charlie felt anxious about her impulse to bring a stranger home. What if Mum was as rude as she'd been to Sean? What if she spoke only in monosyllables, or retreated into her office?

She needn't have worried. Kathy was fascinated by Dietmar, and the fragments of his story gabbled by Charlie in confused order. After showing him the nursery, Kathy offered coffee; Dietmar accepted, and they all sat at the garden table, with Caspar lying underneath.

'So you planted our Frühlingsmorgen rose?' Kathy

asked him. 'We wondered about it.'

'Yes, I planted it as my own memorial for my father. My mother has one also in her garden in Hamburg, bought at the same time. They are twins,' Dietmar said. 'I'm delighted to see how it thrives. It is in good hands, here.' He looked round at the exuberant borders, the veronicas and hardy geraniums that spilled over on to the grass.

'I can't take much credit,' Kathy told him. 'We've only been here since February. Someone else did most of this planting.' She looked at him. 'You? Are you a gardener?'

Dietmar nodded. 'Not an expert like yourself. But I like to dibble.'

'Do you mean dabble?' Charlie couldn't help asking. 'Or is that ducks?'

Kathy laughed. 'No, dibble! *Dibble* – to dibble – means to make holes for planting. With a trowel.' She mimed.

'Then I think I meant dabble,' Dietmar said. 'To try a little bit, to enjoy, yes? But dibble is right too, by accident. I'm sorry, my English is still not yet fully proficient. Even after so many years. You must correct me when I make mistakes.'

'It's a lot better than my German,' Charlie said, thinking that anyone who knew words like *thrives* and *proficient* must surely be entitled to consider himself fluent.

'You're more than just a dabbler,' Kathy said, 'if you did this planting. Have some more coffee?' She proffered the jug. 'So the name *Flightsend* came from you? We wondered what it meant, didn't we, Charlie?'

'Yes. Flightsend.' Dietmar's face became serious. 'The tragic end to my father's flight, and – I thought then – a happy ending to my own flight, my search for a home, a special place. I thought I would settle here.'

'Why didn't you?' Charlie asked. She sensed a reproving look from her mother: *too blunt*.

Dietmar picked up his coffee mug, paused, put it down again. 'I lived here for three years. It didn't turn out quite as I planned. I was living alone for the first time—'

Caspar's ears twitched, he scrambled to his feet and barked, and Charlie saw two people walking into the yard. 'I'll go,' she told her mother.

They were customers, wanting herbs. They took some time deciding. Charlie sold them two varieties of fennel and a French lavender, then went back to the garden, disappointed to see Dietmar on his feet and making signs of leaving.

'Oh, you're going?'

'I'm beginning to feel anxious about the Cessna,' he explained. 'I must go, I think, and remove myself before an angry farmer comes along. But' – he turned to Kathy – 'I'd very much like to have a closer look at your plant nursery some other time. You are open for customers?'

'Yes, every day. Do come again,' Kathy said.

Dietmar shook hands with both of them. 'It was delightful to meet you. Thank you for your hospitality.'

'It's been such a surprise,' Kathy said. 'And we've never had a visitor arrive by plane before.'

They went with him to the gate and watched him wave and turn the corner. Then Kathy said, 'What a nice man. Interesting.'

'Yes,' Charlie said, half-relieved that her mother hadn't turned on her with recriminations. 'I wonder why he left here? Did he say?'

'No, not really. Just that it didn't work out.'

'I heard that bit. What else did he say?' They turned back to the cottage.

'Nothing much. Only that he works at Leicester University, as a senior technician. Apart from that we were talking about the village fête. And delphiniums.'

'He left six years ago, anyway, he told me that,' Charlie said. 'And I suppose he must have sold it to those mad people?'

'*What* mad people?'

'The people who lived here before us. They used to sunbathe in the garden with no clothes on and knit their own sweaters from hand-spun Jacob's sheep wool that absolutely stank. And they used to play Gregorian chants on their stereo all the time, with the volume turned right up.'

Kathy looked incredulous. 'How do you know all that?'

'From Henrietta in the shop. I forgot to tell you.'

'Well, even if they did do those things, it doesn't make them *mad*. I'd expect Henrietta – *and* you – to have a little more tolerance,' Kathy said in what

138

Charlie called her schoolmarm voice. 'There's nothing wrong with eccentricity.'

'Oh! Sean said that!' Charlie exclaimed. 'The same thing exactly. About Henrietta.'

'Did he?' her mother said flatly.

Charlie expected her to say more about Dietmar, but she went straight back to the polytunnel. Wondering if there was anything for lunch, Charlie went indoors to look; but before long, hearing the aircraft engine, she came outside again. She saw the plane – frail and white against the sky – as it swept round in a wide, ascending arc. In case Dietmar was looking down, she stood waving until the churchyard yew trees blocked the plane from sight.

Birthday

Charlie looked after Rosie on Tuesday afternoon, and again on Thursday. It was fairly undemanding, and less fraught with tension than working in the kitchen. Rosie was a good-natured child, easily amused; Charlie read her stories, took her for a walk in the gardens, played a game with building blocks. With Rosie as an excuse, she made a thorough exploration of the grounds, finding areas she hadn't known about. At the farthest end, hidden by the strip of orchard, there was a pond or small lake, fringed with trees.

'Look, Rosie, ducks. Next time, we'll bring some stale bread from the kitchen. And there's a coot,' Charlie said, pointing.

'Toot,' Rosie said obligingly. She was at the stage of labelling everything she saw: *tat* for cat, *Tarlie* for Charlie.

Fay, pleased with Kathy's designs, told Charlie that she was planning to spend more on the gardens. 'We could reclaim that whole pond area. Open it up, have another seating area down there.'

She and Dan had just heard that their National Lottery bid had been successful; they were getting a grant for the improvements. Nightingales was doing well. Dan placed more advertisements in magazines and started planning a smarter brochure for next year, with ink drawings and colour photographs. He commissioned a photographer, and Oliver Locke agreed to do the artwork.

'He'll get on with them once the school term finishes,' Dan told Charlie.

She was annoyed with herself for feeling a definite rush of pleasure at this news; she wasn't sure that she hadn't blushed. If Oliver was doing the brochure drawings, he'd be around at Nightingales without tutoring responsibilities. She had no intention of getting a stupid crush on him, just because he praised her work, but nevertheless she felt that something was missing this week, without him. And, if asked, she'd have known exactly how many days it was to his next weekend course.

She did a few sketches, including one of the rose arch he'd drawn; she went up to the airfield and drew the ash tree and the cross. At home, when her mother was occupied with the nursery, she worked on several drawings of Caspar. It was Kathy's birthday on Saturday, and Charlie had the idea of getting one of the drawings framed and mounted for a present. Progress was difficult, as when Caspar wasn't asleep he was full of twitchy movement. The only drawing she'd completed was of Caspar stretched flat out, asleep, but she knew there was something wrong with it. He was floating in mid-air, rather than lying firmly on the floor. Oliver would know how to put it right, but she wouldn't be seeing him in time, before Saturday.

On Thursday evening she enticed Caspar up to her room, gave him one of his rubber toys to gnaw, and worked hard on a crayon drawing. She was pleased with the result. It was a head-and-front-paws portrait, catching Caspar's endearing way of lying with his front legs crossed as he held the toy against his chest. She perfected his eyebrows, the worried expression in his eyes, and spent some time working on the texture of his fur. When she'd finished, she rolled the picture, with a spare sheet for protection, into a cardboard tube and put it into her rucksack for tomorrow. The leavers' business would be over by lunchtime, and there'd be plenty of time to go into town.

With her school routine broken by study leave, it felt strange to be standing by the village hall with the few other students from the village who travelled in by bus. No more school uniform, either – the sixth form didn't wear it. Rowan had phoned last night to ask Charlie what she'd be wearing.

'Haven't thought about it,' Charlie told her.

'Well, when *are* you going to think about it?'

'In the morning, probably.'

Rowan, disbelieving, gave a long explanation of what she was thinking of wearing and why, then asked Charlie to come shopping after finishing at school. 'I need some things for Tenerife.' Charlie, who hadn't

142

seen Rowan since the party, agreed. She wanted to repair the friendship before the summer holidays began properly.

When the bus arrived, Angus David was sitting by himself in the back seat, deep in his copy of *A Midsummer Night's Dream.*

'*Tarry, rash wanton! Am I not thy lord?*' he said sternly, as she approached.

'Come on then. Let's hear it.'

'Thanks.' He thrust the book at her. 'This is awful. I can't get these words to stick in my head and it's the dress rehearsal on Sunday. The day after *tomorrow.* I'll stand there stammering. I'll be the first Oberon ever with a speech impediment.'

He looked particularly tough today, with hair newly stubbled, an American football shirt with a huge number 2 on it, and heavy boots. 'I thought it was own clothes today,' Charlie teased, 'not fancy dress. Why have you come as Arnold Schwarzenegger?'

Angus tilted his head and looked at her sternly. 'If you were due to appear before the entire school in green tights and a hip-length split tunic, you might want to establish your masculinity first.' He took the book back and turned quickly through the pages to a place marked in yellow highlighter. 'The beginning's all right – here's the part I get stuck on. Ready? You're Puck, by the way. *This is thy negligence: still thou mistak'st, Or else commit'st thy knaveries wilfully* – Bad for the false teeth, that bit.'

In spite of his mock panic, he was almost

word-perfect. 'You must have been out first ball, in the cricket,' Charlie said, 'if you've had time to learn all this.'

'I was not! I got a creditable eighteen runs, since you ask.'

There was a holiday atmosphere at school, and a certain smugness in standing outside talking to friends while rows of younger pupils could be seen, through the windows of the Maths block, having lessons as usual. The official leaving business was an anti-climax. They returned their textbooks, heard a dull and worthy address from the head of year eleven and the head teacher, had coffee and biscuits in the main hall, talked about holiday plans and what they'd do on results day. Some of the teachers came in to chat and to say goodbye. Charlie scanned the room for glimpses of either Oliver or Sean; seeing neither, she was half-disappointed, half-relieved.

Afterwards, in town, she made Rowan come to the art shop before being let loose in Monsoon and Oasis. The framing would normally take two or three days, the assistant told Charlie, but when she explained that the picture was for a present tomorrow he agreed to do it this afternoon. With no need to hurry, Charlie went into Rowan's shop of choice, and watched her trying on a succession of skimpy tops, trousers and dresses.

'What d'you think? Does this colour suit me? Russ would like this. Why don't you get something, Charlie? I mean, you must *need* clothes, even for Nightingales.'

'Clothes don't suit me,' Charlie said. The clingy vests and skirts Rowan liked might have been made for a different species. 'I'd look like a weight-lifter in that dress.'

'There are larger sizes,' Rowan said helpfully. 'What about this?' She pulled out something from the rack of discarded garments at the changing room exit.

'Ro, that's a maternity dress. For an elephant. Either that or something made from a barrage balloon. I don't need anything, thanks.'

Charlie was hungry again. It was no good looking at size 10 clothes; her body would always demand food and let her down. She'd resigned herself to that, but when Rowan made her wait about in changing rooms she developed an inferiority complex, seeing herself as a Great White Whale. She caught a glimpse in one of the many-angled mirrors, and shook out her hair: her fantastic pre-Raphaelite hair, as Mum described it, that people paid vast sums to imitate.

Rowan, posing with hands on hips, looked past her reflection at Charlie. 'I've got an appointment at *Shapers* in half an hour,' she said. 'Why don't you see if they can fit you in too?'

'Oh, so there's something wrong with my hair now?' Charlie retorted. 'And you didn't tell me you were getting yours cut. What am I supposed to do, sit and watch?'

'You could read the magazines.'

'No thanks. I've got more shopping to do. I want to

get some earrings for Mum, an extra birthday present.'

'You didn't say. I'd have helped you choose. Come and meet me outside *Shapers* afterwards.'

Rowan, laden by this time with three carrier-bags, went off to the hairdresser's, and Charlie went to the market stall that sold the kind of ethnic jewellery her mother liked. She chose a pair of delicate silver earrings, browsed in the market for a while and was wondering whether to buy a sandwich when she saw Sean coming out of the outdoor shop.

'Sean!' she called.

He stopped, saw her, came over. 'Charlie! Saw you in school this morning. How was it?'

'Boring. What are you doing?'

'Just bought myself a new compass for Snowdonia.' He showed her. 'And wasted time looking at all the outdoor gear I can't afford. Actually, I'm here for the same reason as you, most likely.'

'Waiting for Rowan to get her hair cut?'

'Kathy's birthday,' he explained. 'What are you getting her?'

Charlie told him about the drawing of Caspar and showed him the earrings. She felt anxious at the implication that he'd be bringing Mum a present, although he wasn't carrying anything other than the compass. Maybe he'd bought jewellery, something small, that was in his pocket. 'Are you coming over tomorrow?' she asked, not wanting him rebuffed again. 'I mean, she – well, it's the village fête. She'll be busy.'

She saw from the twist of his mouth that he understood. 'No, it's all right,' he said. 'I'm sending something. Don't tell her, will you?'

'Course not.'

Sean looked at his watch. 'I've got half an hour, then double year nine this afternoon. Fancy a quick drink and a sandwich? I'm starving.'

'Great!'

They went to *The White Horse* in the market square. It was noisy, packed with office-workers for someone's leaving do.

'Let's sit outside,' said Sean. 'Can't hear ourselves think in here.'

He bought drinks – Coke for Charlie, beer for himself – and led the way through to a garden set out with picnic tables. A barman brought the sandwiches they'd ordered. While they ate, Charlie told Sean about her drawings and her switch to Art, the surprise visit from Dietmar and the story of the wartime plane crash.

'Is Kathy doing anything special for her birthday? Apart from the village fete?' Sean asked.

'She's going out for dinner with Anne. She said I could go too, but I'll be working.'

'You said she was doing some work for Nightingales. How's that going?'

'Really well. They liked what she did, and now they're asking for more plans. She enjoys it, too. Fay said she might even ask Mum to tutor some weekend courses on gardening.'

After a while Charlie noticed that she was doing nearly all the talking, with Sean saying little. He finished his beer but left part of his sandwich uneaten. She wondered if she'd said too much; made it sound as though her mother was having a marvellous time without him. Then she realized: it was almost exactly a year since Sean had moved out, a few days after Kathy's thirty-seventh birthday. He must be thinking of that. The anniversary.

'Have another drink?' she asked. She could give him the money even if she couldn't go to the bar and order it.

'No, thanks, Charlie.' He looked at his watch. 'I ought to get going.'

They went outside. Sean said, 'You know, it's ridiculous. I hardly ever go out of school at lunchtime, and when I do I'm all on edge, watching the clock. Sorry. I wasn't very good company.'

'I'm glad I saw you, anyway,' Charlie said.

'Where are you going now?'

'Back to the art shop.'

'I'd love to see that picture some time,' Sean said. 'It sounds great. Well – have a good day tomorrow.'

They would part here: Charlie going to the art shop in the High Street, Sean back to school. He looked so wistful that when he moved towards the customary embrace, she gave him a big bear hug in return.

He laughed. 'Whoa, steady. What's that for?'

'You looked sad.'

'Oh, not really. I'm OK. See you, Charleston.'

He set off at a jog. Charlie watched him go, then wandered along the High Street. She still had two hours to find a use for, as there was no way back to Lower Radbourne apart from the school bus.

It was only when she got home with the framed drawing wrapped in a parcel that she remembered Rowan, and their arrangement to meet outside the hairdresser's.

Mum's birthday last year, for all Sean's and Charlie's efforts, had been dismal.

It had been on a Friday. After school, Sean and Charlie cooked a surprise special meal; for Saturday they were planning a visit to Hidcote Manor, a National Trust garden Kathy particularly wanted to see.

None of it had gone right. Sean and Charlie didn't have much cooking expertise between them and their choices were too ambitious. The chilli sauce was too hot, the rice turned out gluey and the soufflé didn't rise properly. None of that would have mattered if there hadn't been an item on the radio, just before the meal, about cot deaths. Had she heard it in time, Charlie would have switched to something light-hearted or put a CD on instead. As it was, she came out of the kitchen with a bundle of knives and forks and found her mother huddled in a corner, listening intently.

Charlie didn't tell Sean, who was trying to rescue the rice, filling the kitchen with clouds of steam. As soon as Kathy went upstairs, Charlie turned off the radio and found a CD, but it was too late to salvage the evening. Kathy toyed with the food on her plate, hardly spoke, drank her wine half-heartedly. When Sean got up to make coffee, she said, 'I don't want any, thanks. I've got a headache. I think I'll have an early night.'

Charlie and Sean cleared up in near-silence. Mum's depression was like a virus, infecting all three of them. No amount of cheerful determination from Sean could hide the signs that his relationship with Kathy was foundering, and he could do nothing to save it. Charlie knew by now that adults might give all sorts of advice about problems and relationships, but that didn't mean they could sort out their own lives.

Putting away glasses, she came across the birthday cake Sean had hidden in the cupboard. They'd planned to bring it out with the coffee. The candles – pink and white, pathetic now – were already in place, a box of matches nearby.

'Oh, the *cake*!' Charlie exclaimed.

Sean shrugged. 'Chuck it in the bin, for all I care. Drink your coffee, now I've made it.'

Tears stung Charlie's eyes, welled up. She gulped at her coffee, which he'd made much stronger than she liked it. Then she remembered that Sean didn't know about the radio item. Thinking it might help to explain her mother's behaviour, she told him.

'What?' He stared at her. 'Why didn't you turn it off? Why didn't you *tell* me?'

'Didn't want to spoil the whole evening.'

'It's spoiled all right, isn't it? I'm going up to talk to her.' He left the cooking dish he'd been scrubbing and went upstairs.

Charlie poured the rest of her coffee down the sink and finished tidying, leaving the dish to soak. Then she turned off the lights and went up, too. Getting ready for bed, she heard muttered words from the other bedroom: Sean's voice, low and pleading; her mother's, irritable at first, becoming angry. Finally, 'Oh, leave me alone, *please*! Just leave me alone!'

Charlie heard Sean come out and go to the bathroom, then his footsteps going downstairs. The sofa creaked as he settled on it.

Wide awake by now and staring into the darkness, she thought of the nursery, perfect and untouched behind its closed door. There were three people in the house, sleepless and miserable, lying isolated in their separate rooms. It needed the tiny, absent fourth person to unite them. Without Rose, they were identical magnet poles, repelling each other.

Village Fête

Fay had asked Charlie to spend Saturday afternoon at Nightingales, serving refreshments for the village fête, but Charlie had already promised to help her mother. On Kathy's birthday, Charlie wanted to be with her; she felt a duty to watch out for signs of disaster.

It was a beautiful, fresh morning. Charlie got up early to take her mother tea in bed before going round to Nightingales, but when she went downstairs she found Kathy already out on the lawn in her dressing-gown. She was looking at a clematis that had just come into flower.

'Happy birthday, Mum.' Charlie kissed her and gave her the mug of tea. 'You're invited to a presentation ceremony, to be held in the kitchen in five minutes.'

'Thanks, Charlie. Look at this – *clematis viticella* Étoile Violette. Isn't it gorgeous?' She touched one of the curving purple blooms. 'Flowering for my birthday.'

She put on the earrings as soon as she'd unwrapped them, and was delighted with the picture of Caspar.

'I'll hang it today. Above the fireplace, do you think that's the best place? I'll do it before the fête, if there's time.'

So far, so good, Charlie thought. She went off to do her Nightingales breakfast shift, and came back just before ten to find a florist's delivery van outside, with the driver taking a huge sheaf of lilies to the front door.

'I'll take them,' Charlie said, guessing that they were from Sean. He knew that Kathy loved lilies. She carried them, crackling in their cellophane wrapping, round to the yard, where her mother was busy sorting plants for the fête. The scent was intoxicating. The lilies were beautiful: white, with deep pink speckled markings.

Her mother was assembling plants in plastic crates: herbs, hardy geraniums, penstemons. 'Special delivery,' Charlie said, presenting the bouquet with a flourish.

Kathy straightened, saw the lilies. Her eyes widened. 'Oh, how lovely! From Anne, I suppose. Is there a message?'

She reached inside the wrapping and took out a tiny card in an envelope. Charlie watched closely. Kathy read it, said nothing and tucked it inside the cellophane, against the lily stems.

'Well?' Charlie asked.

'From Sean,' her mother said. 'I'll arrange them in a minute.'

'Aren't they fantastic?' Charlie tried.

'Yes, wonderful. Stirling Star, I think.'

Charlie, hoping for some expression of gratitude towards the sender – even a bland *how kind* or *what a nice thought* – was disappointed. She took Caspar out for a quick walk, passing the village green where stalls were already being set out, and spent the rest of the morning helping her mother with the packing, labelling and pricing of the plants. Taking some empty compost-bags round to the dustbin, she saw the card from the flowers discarded inside with its envelope and the cellophane wrapping.

Charlie couldn't resist turning it over.

There was a small coloured illustration of irises, and *For Kathy, on your birthday*, written in Sean's distinctive, angular handwriting. *I love you. Sean.*

Charlie's hand trembled as she picked up the card and slipped it into her jeans pocket. Her head was spinning with anger at her mother, all tangled up with bitter disappointment on Sean's behalf. How *could* she? How could she read that and sling it aside with the rubbish? It made it worse, somehow, that Kathy was usually so punctilious about recycling paper and card. Sean's message wasn't worth even that to her. She didn't want to soil her hands with it, couldn't wait to bin it. She hadn't even bothered hiding it. It was so *stupid*, Charlie thought – Mum convinced that Sean wanted to find someone his own age, wanted to enjoy being young and single, whereas Sean, a whole year after she'd kicked him out, still wasn't giving up.

What had Mum done to deserve such loyalty, such devotion?

Charlie was too upset to confront her mother. If she let herself speak, she'd end up shouting harsh, unforgivable things. Not today. Avoiding Kathy, she went into the office and sat there writing labels in indelible pen.

The fête was a success. The warm weather brought people out in numbers, and Henrietta – in a bizarre ankle-length garment in a bold African print and even more clanking jewellery than usual – went from stall to stall, beaming encouragement. Kathy and Charlie, too busy with customers to have much time to speak to each other, sold so many plants that Kathy went back to Flightsend for more. Besides the stalls and refreshments, there were additional attractions: a fortune-teller (friend of Henrietta's), jugglers, acrobats and a tug-of-war, and the Long Wykham Morris dancers. The accordion player was already practising a few snatches, adding to the fairground atmosphere.

When Anne Gladwin arrived unexpectedly and offered to help, Kathy sent Charlie to have a look round. A crowd was gathering round the Morris-men, so Charlie followed the drift and was astonished to see, hopping and skipping among them, Angus David. She did a double-take. Yes, Angus, in a flowered straw hat, garters with jingling bells, sturdy calves in white socks, feet stamping in clumpy shoes. During the next dance he and three others took a break, while a smaller number of dancers performed a routine with clashing sticks. Charlie went over to him.

'Another of your talents? Is there anything you can't do?'

Angus was red in the face under his straw hat, from exertion or embarrassment. He took off the hat and fanned himself with it.

'Andy Ferris sprained his ankle last weekend, falling off a ladder. I'm the stand-in.'

'The dairying spin-bowler? Don't tell me – you're milking his cows as well?'

'No, there are limits. I've had a week of practice but I'm still winging it. This stick-bashing stuff I leave to the experts. Too much risk of knuckle damage.'

'All that *and* the rehearsals?'

'Dress rehearsal tomorrow,' Angus told her. 'If you've got time for a bit of *ill-met by moonlight, proud Titania,* I've come prepared.' He pulled a battered copy of *A Midsummer Night's Dream* from the back pocket of his trousers.

'I would, but I'm helping Mum,' Charlie explained, gesturing towards the plant stall.

'Aha!' Angus said, looking. 'She might be just the person. We need vegetation. *I know where the wild thyme blows,*' he explained. 'Come on, Charlie, do keep up.'

'Angus!' one of the Morris-men called.

'OK, so it's my turn to keep up. *The Sheep-Shearer's Ditty,* or some such.'

'Aren't there any Morris-*women*?' Charlie asked.

'Great Oaksett's got a women's team, if you're interested. Or was that an Equality of Opportunity question?'

'Yes, it was. Don't forget your hat.'

Charlie watched for a while. Angus danced as he did everything, with great precision and comic seriousness. She joined in the clapping before going back to the stall.

'Was that Angus David in the hat and bells?' asked Anne, who had been his History teacher.

'Yes! Go and watch. He's so funny.'

'OK, while it's quiet.'

Henrietta was approaching the plant stall, talking animatedly to a man in a cream jacket. 'You two,' she said importantly to Kathy and Charlie. 'I must introduce you to someone who used to live in your cottage.'

The man with her was Dietmar.

'Oh, we've already met,' Kathy said. 'Hello, Dietmar! How nice to see you again.' She looked around as if expecting to see the aircraft.

'No Cessna today,' Dietmar said, laughing. He shook hands with her and with Charlie. 'I came by car.'

'Specially for the village fête,' Kathy asked, 'or . . .?'

'Specially for the village fête,' Dietmar said. 'I am hoping the WI cake stall is keeping up its high standards. But now I am going to buy some of your plants.' He was one of those men, Charlie noticed, who looked stylish even in casual summer clothes. She only had to look around at the baggy shorts and stomachs bulging under T-shirts to see what a mess the average British male made of it. Surely, she thought, he hasn't driven all the way from Leicester just to buy cakes and plants?

'When you've finished, don't forget to visit Madame Sosostris,' Henrietta told him. 'She's in the tent by the tombola.'

'Thank you, but I won't risk it,' Dietmar said. 'I might be afraid of what she tells me.'

Henrietta looked unsure whether to take the remark seriously. Then she looked critically at the red T-shirt Charlie was wearing again. 'I hope you won't forget to look at my clothes, Charlie.'

Charlie, thinking Henrietta meant the bold African thing she had on, thought she was being asked for a compliment. 'Oh, it's . . . er . . .'

But Henrietta was pointing to her own stall, next to the tombola. 'Special bargains today,' Henrietta said. 'And there are *green* bargains, just for you. I do find that red so terribly distressing on you, with your colouring. That's my friend Jiminy, in the skull cap, manning the stall for me. Tell him I sent you.'

Then, distracted by someone asking about toilets, she moved on. Dietmar spent a long time choosing plants and eventually chose three hardy geraniums, one of which he said reminded him of the garden at Flightsend. Then he asked if he could buy Charlie and her mother a cup of tea.

'You go, Mum,' Charlie said. 'I'll look after these.' She wrote DIETMAR on the carrier bag the plants were in, and stowed it under the table. 'Teas are round the corner, at Nightingales, the big house,' she told him. 'You can buy her a piece of cake as well – it's her birthday.' Her mother would enjoy talking to Dietmar; while he'd been making up his mind, they'd got well into propagation techniques and colour combinations and plants that flowered at that difficult time in late summer.

'Charlie!' Kathy reproved.

'Really? Then I wish you many happy returns,' Dietmar said, in his formal way. 'In that case, tea seems definitely in order, if you would accompany me?'

Angus, Anne, Dietmar – who else was going to turn up? Charlie had wondered whether Sean might come, and was half-disappointed that he hadn't; but perhaps he wouldn't risk being spurned in public. And it was probably just as well he wasn't here. Charlie couldn't help comparing the warmth of the reception Dietmar had just been given with the cool treatment her mother handed out to Sean. She knew that Kathy wouldn't even phone to thank Sean for the lilies.

Anne returned with three ice-cream cornets. 'Oh, where's Kathy gone?'

'She's gone to have tea with a German pilot,' Charlie said.

'With a *what*?'

'With Dietmar Kolbert of Hamburg and Leicester via Flightsend. I'll tell you in a minute.' Charlie eyed the cornets, that were starting to drip. 'Should we eat those first?'

Charlie had known Anne for years – before even starting at Westbury Park. Anne had been her mother's best friend through the Sean time, through the baby time. She'd been living with someone, then, when that broke up, had lived alone for some while. Now, she had a part-time relationship with a man in Newcastle-on-Tyne, seeing him on alternate weekends. Charlie liked Anne, both as Mum's friend and at school. She was quietly-spoken, always unflappably calm. Once, upset by a bullying campaign against a newcomer at school, Charlie had told Anne, who, without involving Charlie again or causing the least embarrassment, had firmly sorted it out. She was good at dealing with problems, and knew Kathy better than anyone.

'Anne,' Charlie said, when they'd finished all three ice creams and put out more plants, and she'd explained about Dietmar, 'listen – Mum will kill me if she knows I've told you this, but . . .'

She told Anne about Sean, last week's visit, the lilies and the thrown-away card. Inevitably, two customers came up and spent ages dithering between two different colours of scabious. When at last they'd gone, Charlie put their money into the cash-box and appealed: 'Don't you think she's being unreasonable?'

Anne sorted out notes and laid them in the bottom of the box, underneath the coin trays.

'It must seem like that,' she said slowly, 'but she's got to do it her own way. It's hard for you and it's hard for Sean, but I think he's got to take no for an answer.'

'Oh, but . . .'

This wasn't what Charlie wanted to hear. Anne knew Sean well; Charlie expected her to take his side, to agree that yes, Kathy was behaving outrageously, and if she had any sense she'd phone Sean this instant and beg him to come back.

'She's so determined to make this new start. I admire her for it,' Anne said. 'It takes guts to make such a complete break, giving up her job and moving out here. How many people stay in jobs they don't like, year after year, just because they can't take the plunge?'

'I don't mind about the *job*,' Charlie said. 'She could have given that up and moved out here and still not split with Sean. Why won't she even meet him in a friendly way? He deserves that, doesn't he?'

'But the reason she won't be friendly is that it's too risky for her,' Anne said. 'You realize that? She's afraid of giving in, if she sees too much of him. And she doesn't want to give way just because she feels sorry for him. That wouldn't work.'

'But why should it *be* like that?'

Anne looked at her. 'Because it just is. You can't tell people how to feel. I hated it when they split up – as much as you did. I wasn't sure Kathy really knew what she was doing. Also, I like Sean, a lot, and I hated to see him so devastated. But it's happened, and that's her decision, and they've both got to get on with their lives. She's doing all right, Charlie. You've heard of people getting post-natal depression – well, hers was a hundred times worse, with no baby. But she's picking herself up. It's taking time, but she's doing it. And if there's no place for Sean, he'll have to accept it. After all, if she's giving him no encouragement but he keeps making these approaches – well, he must know by now what response he's likely to get.'

Charlie said nothing. She rearranged some of the plant pots and straightened a label.

'He'll get over it, in time,' Anne said. 'He'll have to. And – you're a terrific help, Charlie. I'm so glad she's got you. It's tough for you, too, but you're mature and sensible and you're giving her a lot of support. She appreciates it.'

'Oh, yeah,' Charlie grumped. 'I've noticed.'

'Well, she's always telling *me* how good you are. How she'd fall apart without you. Here comes Angus, so I'm going to stop talking like an agony aunt,' Anne said. 'Well done, Angus! Have you finished Morrissing for the day?'

Angus trudged over heavily, feigning exhaustion. 'Yeah, we're off in a minute. Coming to the barn dance tonight, Charlie?'

'Can't, I'm working,' Charlie said, 'but if it's still going on when I've finished, I'll come on my way back.'

'OK, see you later, then.'

'I didn't know you were a Morris-man. Or a barn dancer. Any other surprises?' Anne said, and then, when he'd performed a few steps and twirls and gone back to the other dancers, 'He's great, isn't he?'

'He's an idiot – a nice one,' Charlie said. 'He doesn't care what anyone thinks – he just does what he wants. Oh, here's Mum. They've been ages.'

Kathy, still with Dietmar in tow, came across the trodden grass. 'Sorry! I hope you didn't mind being left for so long,' she said. 'We keep meeting people Dietmar knew when he lived here. And we've been over to Henrietta's stall and she said I had to buy you this.' She handed Charlie a soft, floppy bag. Charlie shook out what was inside: a long batik top, light and floaty, in a greeny-gold colour. She held it up.

'Thanks, Mum! It's lovely. Henrietta's been going on at me to get this. But you're the one with the birthday – you should have bought something for yourself.'

'No, I wanted to buy you a present,' Kathy said seriously. 'For helping. Thank you.'

Charlie noticed Anne's face registering *I told you so* smugness because of the present, and Mum looking animated, even excited.

'Oh, sorry,' Kathy said. 'You two don't know each other, do you? Anne, Dietmar, who used to live in our house – Dietmar, my friend Anne. Dietmar's just offered to give me the most fantastic birthday present—'

Rosie

'You could at least have *phoned*.' Rowan's disgruntlement came through the receiver loud and clear. 'To say you were *sorry*.'

'Yes, I know. I was going to and then I forgot,' Charlie said.

'Forgot to phone? As well as forgetting to come back for me?'

'Sorry, but I did. I've been busy.'

'Oh, *that's* all right then,' Rowan huffed. 'Too busy to pick up a phone? Anyway, it didn't matter about Friday. Russell came and found me at *Shapers*.'

'Good. I'm really glad you didn't have to walk home all by yourself.'

'*Charlie*,' Rowan said, on a warning upward note. 'Anyway, Russell thinks my new hair's great. You should have come to Jason's party last night. I did ask. Too many early nights are bad for you, you know.'

'I didn't go to bed early. I went to the village barn dance. For the last hour, anyway, after work.'

'Village *barn* dance,' Rowan said scathingly. 'Well, I bet that was a rave. What was it, cowboy boots and yee-hahs?'

'Actually, it was fun. Much better than some tedious party where everyone thinks they're cool.'

'So who did you dance with? Some local pig-farmer?'

'I danced with Angus,' Charlie said. 'And with Dan from Nightingales, and Oliver Locke, and two other people I don't know.'

'Angus, King of the Fairies? Careful, you'll start rumours. You're not going *out* with him, are you?'

'Course not,' Charlie said loftily. 'Can't I have two dances with someone in the village hall without people thinking we're an item?'

'*Two dances.* Well, there you are. In *Pride and Prejudice*, when Mr Bingley danced twice with Jane, it was practically a way of announcing their engagement. Wait, Mr Locke, did you say? I might have thought it was worth coming, for that. How many times?'

'Just once.'

'Hey, that's not why you're switching to Art, is it? So you can hang around with Mr Oliver Lush?'

'No, it's *not*,' Charlie said. 'I'm not basing my career options on whether or not I fancy the teacher. That wouldn't give much choice.'

Rowan giggled. 'So when am I going to see you, then?'

'School on Thursday, this sixth-form thing. I'll wait for you by the buses.'

'Right. And don't *forget*, this time.'

Rowan rang off, and Charlie sat on the stairs thinking of yesterday and its various surprises: Angus, the conversation with Anne, the barn dance. Most of all, Dietmar. He was going to take Kathy for a flight in the Cessna, from the flying club in Leicester.

'How *fantastic*,' Anne had said when Kathy told them, providing a cover for Charlie's reaction, an open-mouthed, silent *But* . . .

She thought now of the reasons for that *But.*

But I want to go. I was the one who brought him home. Self-centred, grudging. OK, she could make an effort to eliminate that one.

But it might be dangerous. No. Illogical. Dietmar was a qualified pilot; it was probably safer than driving into town, or crossing the street.

But it's practically going out *with him* . . . Hmm. Was it? What if it was?

But he's so much older than you. You can't go out with a man who's nearly old enough to be my grandfather . . . She wasn't sure about that one. Dietmar was kind, intelligent, interesting; even quite attractive if you didn't mind a certain weathering. It would depend on what happened next, really.

But what about Sean? How can you throw his message in the bin, then the *same day* get all girly and excited when another man asks you to do something?

Yes. That was the real *But.* The others could be got over; that last one couldn't. Charlie kept all her

166

doubts to herself, and even managed to take a polite interest in the plan for the flight. But she was sure by now that Kathy had noticed her pointed silence on the subject of Dietmar.

For the last few days, Charlie had been thinking of drawing a portrait of Rosie.

When Fay next asked her to child-mind, on Monday afternoon, Charlie collected a bagful of toys and objects likely to interest a two-year-old and took her out on the grass, under the mulberry tree. Rosie, in a white sun-hat and a smocked dress, examined the items one by one, discarding some, keeping others close by her.

'Tonker.'

'Conker, Rosie.'

'Tonker. *Two* tonkers.' Rosie reached into the bag. 'Trayon.'

'Crayon.'

'Crayon. Duck. Cortoise.'

'*Tortoise.* Say *tortoise.*'

'Torkoise.'

Sketching the first tentative lines, Charlie saw that Rosie would be a more difficult subject than the models in class. And not only because Rosie wasn't sitting still. Soft, childish flesh and small features were harder to capture than wrinkles and blemishes; Rosie's open-mouthed, absorbed expression was harder to convey than the firmer lines suggestive of character in a mature face. After a while Rosie tired

167

of the animals and toys and cuddled up to Charlie. It was like trying to take a photograph of Caspar, when he kept wanting to lick her face and sniff the camera.

'Tarlie! Tory!'

'All right. I'll tell you a story, if you play with the tortoise and duck while you listen. What story would you like?' Last week, they'd had *Goldilocks and the Three Bears* and *The Three Little Ducks.*

'*Tarlie* tory.'

'All right.' Charlie drew in a tumbling curl of hair while she thought. 'OK. Are you ready? Once upon a time, there was a little girl called – oh, what was her name now? Yes. Rosie. Rosie lived in a big house with her mummy and daddy and two cats called – Sooty and Sweep. Usually Rosie was very good and did as she was told, but one day she was naughty. *Always stay by the house,* her mummy had told her. *Never go down to the big pond on your own.* But Rosie wanted to feed the ducks, so she went to the kitchen and found a big loaf of stale bread. When her mummy wasn't looking, she crept off down the garden and went down to the big pond.'

Rosie was looking at her, round-eyed, with a finger in her mouth.

'Yes, it was naughty, wasn't it? You see, Rosie, it was a *very* big pond, much bigger and much further away than yours is here. Much too far for a little girl to go on her own. The water was very black and deep and there were big fish in the depths. When Rosie

168

got there, she broke up the bread into little pieces and threw it to the ducks, but no ducks came. Rosie began to feel frightened. She looked into the water and thought . . .' Charlie paused, drawing Rosie's small rounded nose.

'Fall in,' Rosie contributed.

'Yes, that's right. She might fall in, and there was no one to jump in and save her. She tried to remember what her mummy had told her. What did her mummy say?'

'*Don't go to the tond. Stay by house.*'

'Very good. You see, you're much better at remembering than the Rosie in the story. By now she really *did* want to go back home, but she'd walked round the pond and there were lots of different paths leading off, and she wasn't sure which way was home.'

Rosie shook her head knowingly. 'Lost.'

'That's right, she was lost. So she walked all the way round the pond trying to see if she could find the path home. There were thick, dark trees and bushes growing close to the edge, and as Rosie passed them she heard a voice calling to her—'

'Mummy!'

'No, it wasn't her mummy. Nor her daddy. It was a voice she hadn't heard before. It said, "Come with me, Rosie. Come home with me. Come and live with me and my – my husband." This poor lady had always wanted a little girl like Rosie, a little girl of her own to love, but she didn't have one. "Come with me, Rosie," she called again. "Come home to my cottage. There's a lovely bedroom all ready for you with a soft, warm bed, and there's plenty of food, there's – oh – lots of chocolate and ice-cream and maple syrup pancakes and bananas, and there's a big teddy bear with a red spotted bow-tie who's just waiting to be cuddled. All this is waiting for you, Rosie, if you come with me."'

Rosie's eyes were fixed on Charlie's face, her mouth slightly open.

'No, Rosie shouldn't go with her, should she? I think Rosie knew that. But you see, this lady was sad, not bad, because she really, really wanted Rosie to go and live with her. More than anything in the world, she wanted a little girl of her own—'

What am I *doing*? Charlie thought. She stopped drawing to sharpen her pencil. The strange freedom of story-telling was making her speak faster than she was thinking. Where was this taking her?

Rosie was waiting, rapt and attentive.

'So what did Rosie do?' Charlie asked. 'Well, she was a good little girl really, and she remembered that her mummy had told her never, ever to go off with someone she didn't know, so she ran very fast all the way home. Oh, no, she couldn't have! She didn't know which way to go, did she? But just as she was wondering, she heard Sooty and Sweep miaowing in the bushes. She called them, and they trotted out to meet her and showed her the way home. And Rosie's mummy made her scrambled egg on toast for tea, and afterwards they had jam doughnuts and raspberry milkshake. And that's the end of the story. What shall we call it?'

'Don't know.'

'I know. *Rosie's Walk*,' Charlie said, because Rosie had the picture book *Rosie's Walk*. 'This is *Rosie's Other Walk*.'

'Lady?' Rosie said, in the very serious, deliberate way she had.

'What about her? Did she ever get a little girl of her own?' Charlie thought for a moment. 'No. No, she didn't.'

Rosie looked so disappointed that Charlie added, 'But soon she met a very nice hamster. In fact, *two* hamsters, called Herbert and Hilary. They were looking for a home, and the lady had plenty of room. So Herbert and Hilary moved in, and the lady and her husband were very happy. And now, shall we go and feed the ducks? We'll go and see Jon and get some bread. Because you're allowed to go down to the pond when you're with me, and I won't forget the way home.'

She would finish the drawing later. It wasn't really working; too much had gone into the story. She collected her things together and piled the toys back into the bag.

Later that evening, after Kathy had gone to bed, Charlie sat at the kitchen table and took out the sketch. She looked at it for some while before picking up her pencil, loth to spoil it. Then, as soon as she began, she worked intently. She never knew how it would be: sometimes she just fiddled, really starting. At other times – now – energy flowed down her arm and into the tip of the pencil.

There was no Charlie in the story, she thought. I left out Charlie.

She began to think of a new version.

Once upon a time, there was a little girl called Rose.

Rose had a mother and a father and a sister, and they all wanted her more than anything in the world. Rose was the precious gift they hoped for and waited for. They made plans for her, they bought her presents, they prepared a room.

They waited and waited, they wanted and wanted, but Rose didn't come. They hoped so much that they frightened her away. She wouldn't be trapped in the warm, comfortable cage they'd built for her. Just as the cage door opened to entice her inside, she skittered away and flew free. She went where they could never find her, no matter how hard they searched. She left no trail for them to follow. When she heard them weeping, she felt sorry, so she took with her a little piece cut out from her mother's heart, and a little piece of her father's, and a little piece of her sister's. She carried those pieces of heart as far as she could, but when they became too heavy she flung them away and they floated out into the sky, beyond the stars, where they froze into solid ice . . .

The child's face in the drawing was rapt, intent on the model tortoise she was gripping in both hands. A hat shaded her face, with stray curls escaping. Her eyelids were lowered, her mouth slightly open.

It wasn't Rosie's face. It was someone else's.

Misinterpretation

They were to be treated as sixth form from today. No uniform, and they were allowed to use the sixth-form common room.

'Wow! A sink and a kettle!' Angus said. 'Now I know why the year twelves look so smug.' He put on a pompous swagger. '*Hey!* I'm in the sixth form and I can make my own coffee. Get out of my way, you insignificant little year-eleven squit.'

'I'll pretend I didn't hear that, Angus,' said Ms Winterbourne, the Head of Sixth Form. 'It's time to move off to your subject areas.'

Each of them had been given an individual timetable. Charlie's programme showed English and History for the morning, with Art in the afternoon. In each of the first two sessions the teacher outlined the course and handed out a list for suggested summer reading. On Thursday and Friday, there would be sample lessons.

The art session in the afternoon was different. There were two groups of students, and two teachers

– Ms Pearson, the Head of Art, and Oliver Locke. All available space in the art rooms was given over at present to the exhibition of work by the year thirteen students, those who'd just finished their course. The new pupils were encouraged to look at the work in detail – not just the framed and mounted pieces, but the sketchbooks, folders and critical studies.

'To do well in this course, you've got to regard yourself as an artist,' Ms Pearson said. 'Don't think of it as lessons and homework. Just as your work. Draw every day. Look. Notice. Experiment.'

Charlie thought: I already do think of myself as an artist, if that's what it means. It had become a habit to draw something every day. If she had to miss a day, she felt feel itchy and restless. She rarely went out without putting her sketchbook and pencils into her rucksack. Comparing herself with some of the others, like Lisa Skillett, who was doing Art because she didn't fancy anything else, Charlie felt a surge of confidence. She could do this.

'Oh God, look,' Lisa was saying, leafing through a critical study on Fauvism, with page after page of elegant italic writing. 'All this *work*. I'll never do it. I'll have to choose something really easy.'

'I've never yet known anyone choose Philip Wilson, Charlie.'

She jumped. She hadn't known Mr Locke was standing behind them.

'Steer by Steer,' he said. 'How about it?'

'I don't know yet. If I chose him, I'd do John Singer Sargent and Gwen John as well.'

He looked pleased. 'You've been reading the book?'

'Yes. It's interesting. I love that painting of Walberswick. Not the girls running. The golden misty one, of the man and the woman looking out at the river and the mud flats and the boats.'

'Mm, I know the one you mean,' Oliver Locke said. 'Come and look at this. Let me show you some stunningly good A-grade work.' He touched her shoulder lightly, guiding her out of the room. Charlie wondered if he meant Lisa to come, too, but Lisa stayed where she was, pulling a sarky face at Charlie behind Oliver's back.

The work he wanted to show her was by Francesca Abbott, a girl Charlie knew by sight. It had been given a prominent position, occupying a whole section of corridor. Folders and notebooks covered two tables. The mounted work was dominated by a large stylised landscape with cypress trees, in pointillist style. Alongside there were several studies of a female nude.

'She's already been accepted for a foundation course. And she'll get an A for sure.'

For the first time, Charlie felt daunted. 'It's brilliant. Miles better than I can do.'

'But not better than you *will* do. Remember she's two years ahead of you.'

Charlie could see what marked out Francesca's work as special: it had the confidence to be what it was. There was no fussing, no hesitancy. She tried to explain this to Oliver, who nodded and said, 'And she understands light. Look at that, the tones of the grass as it recedes into the distance. The colours of the shadows. And here, and here.'

'I'm going to have a really good look at her critical study, and her folder,' Charlie said.

'OK. I'll be interested to hear what you think.'

Oliver left her, and a few moments later Lisa appeared. 'Oo*oo*oo!' she jibed. 'What are you, Locke's special pet? Does he fancy you or something?'

Charlie ignored that. 'Look at this work. Francesca Abbott. Doesn't it make you want to give up now?' she said, although it didn't.

'I'll give up before you do,' Lisa said. 'Francesca Abbott – that's the weird-looking tall girl who gets her clothes from the Oxfam shop?'

'She looks good in them,' Charlie said. 'Different. Like a – well, like an art student, I suppose.'

'She was always down here. I wonder she had time to do any other subjects. Hey, she was *this* year's teacher's pet,' Lisa said. 'You're next.' She frowned at the nude studies. 'Are *we* going to do this? If I had thighs as big as those, and such a scrawny chest, I wouldn't want to sprawl naked in front of a bunch of teenagers, would you?'

Charlie had asked Fay for Thursday night off, so that she could go to *A Midsummer Night's Dream* with Rowan and Russell.

'As long as it's understood that the love interest

177

takes place on the stage, not in the audience,' Charlie specified to Rowan. 'Maybe I'd better sit between you.'

'You can come round after school and have something to eat,' Rowan offered. 'Then you needn't go all the way home and back. My dad can take you home afterwards.' Fortunately, Rowan's dad never seemed to object to her casual way of using him as taxi-driver.

After the last lesson on Thursday, waiting near the front entrance for Rowan, Charlie saw Sean walking back from the athletics track with two of his PE colleagues. She hesitated, wanting to attract his attention without yelling his name in front of the dozens of pupils funnelling out of the side doors. She walked quickly towards the reception door, so that her path crossed his.

'Oh, Charlie . . .'

To her surprise, his smile of greeting turned quickly to a look of edginess. The other two teachers, Mr Wade and Ms Grear, walked on towards the staffroom; Charlie heard Mr Wade complaining: 'And I could have done without losing my one free period, with sports day coming up . . .'

Charlie said to Sean, 'I just wanted to—'

'Yes, we need to talk. But not here.' He lowered his voice. 'PE office, in five minutes? Oh – no, you've got to get your bus.'

'No, it's OK,' Charlie said, mystified. 'I'm not getting the bus.'

Sean nodded, and walked quickly after his colleagues. Charlie, glimpsing Rowan, went to tell her that she'd be a few minutes. She had no idea what Sean could possibly want to tell her. Thinking of Anne, Charlie now half-regretted approaching him. What had she meant to say? How delighted Kathy was with the lilies? With the note?

No. She shouldn't interfere, as her mother had told her on countless occasions. She just wanted to talk to him, that was all.

Sean came along the corridor and unlocked the office. Inside was a muddle of noticeboards and cluttered desks and odd bits of equipment, whistles and a wicket-keeper's glove and a box of rounders bats. He gestured for Charlie to go in, then followed her, leaving the door to the corridor open. He stood facing her, fiddling with his bunch of keys. To fill the rather awkward silence, she said, choosing her words carefully, 'Those lilies are gorgeous. Mum's favourite. They came early on Saturday and she's got them arranged in a vase. They'll last ages.'

Sean gave a short, humourless laugh. 'Yes. Well. I must be incredibly thick-skinned, mustn't I? To keep pestering her.'

'Sean, no!'

'That's how she must see it. Anyway, I didn't mean to talk about Kathy,' he said. 'I wanted to see you first, to warn you – just in case Mr Fletcher says anything. He hasn't, has he?'

'No, about what?'

Mr Fletcher was the head teacher, a remote dark-suited figure rarely seen in a classroom; Charlie had

had no personal contact with him through her entire time at the school, and couldn't imagine why he'd speak to her now.

'He called me into his office this morning,' Sean said.

Charlie looked at him, puzzled. He picked at the leather tab on his key-fob, then said, 'Apparently – you know last Friday, when we went to the pub? Well, someone saw us. A parent. And got the wrong end of the stick. And thought the Head should be told.'

'Got the wrong end of the—' Charlie didn't understand. 'You're entitled to go the pub at lunchtime if you want, surely? As long as you don't come back drunk.'

'No, it's not about having a drink. What this parent saw was a teacher coming out of a pub with a sixteen-year-old student.'

Charlie flushed. She remembered coming out of *The White Horse* with Sean, giving him a hug and a kiss, without a thought that there was anything wrong in it. That was what the parent had seen.

'What business is it of anyone's? Of Mr Fletcher's? What did he say, then? Accuse you of – of—'

'He had to follow it up. If a parent makes an – an allegation like that, he has to at least ask me about it. I think he was a bit embarrassed, to be honest.'

'So what did you say?'

'Well, obviously, I told him it was *you* I was with, and that we're practically family. This parent didn't give your name. Just recognized you as a student of this school, I suppose, or else just assumed. Of course the Head knows Kathy, so once I'd explained, he was quite OK about it. I mean it's not up to him where I go and who I see outside school – he made that clear. But he also said . . .' Sean stopped, frowned.

'What?'

Sean looked at her. 'That it's open to misinterpretation.'

Charlie felt outrage welling up inside her. 'So he *is* telling you where you can go and who you can see!'

'Think about it, Charlie. I lived with you and Kathy for five years but now there's no official relationship between us. What am I? Not your stepfather, not your mum's husband or even partner, any more. I'm only your mum's ex-boyfriend, and that's not enough, really, if people start nosing around. I should have thought. It was an – indiscretion, I suppose. I wanted to tell you first, just in case he decides to warn you, too.'

Charlie thought of politicians caught out in sordid affairs. *Indiscretion*. That was the euphemism they used.

'No! Don't use that word, *indiscretion*! It makes it sound wrong, shameful!' she burst out. 'You bought me a sandwich and a Coke, we talked about Mum's birthday, that was all – we even bumped into each other by accident! I hate the thought of people watching us, thinking horrible suspicious thoughts!'

'I know—'

'Mr Fletcher can warn me if he likes, but what am I supposed to do if I see you in town? Ignore you?

181

Pretend I don't know you?' she flared. 'He ought to get on the phone to that parent and say *Yeah, so what? They know each other, they're friends, and what business is it of yours?*'

'I expect he will, only a bit more politely. The point is,' Sean said, 'he's had the chance to put the bloke right, this time, but what if the parent hadn't phoned? What if he told other parents, spread rumours? Said I was unprofessional, taking advantage of my teacher role?'

'So you're *agreeing* with him? You're telling me I can't speak to you in public in case some nosy parent's watching?'

She thought: this isn't just to warn me about Mr Fletcher. It's to tell me he's going to treat me like any other student.

'No, I'm *not*,' Sean said. 'I'm not going to start ignoring you. I just have to be aware of what people might think.'

'Let them think what they like! *I* don't care – why should you?'

'Because it's different for me. It wouldn't matter if you weren't a student here. You're sixteen, not a child. If we were just two people, no problem. But I'm a teacher, and that means hundreds of people – parents as well as kids – know me by sight. Whenever I go into town I'm recognized. Teachers have to be aware of that. It's a bit like being a social worker or a doctor – you have a professional relationship with people and it's wrong to take advantage.'

'But—'

'You have to be careful not to put yourself in a position where people might *think* you're taking advantage.'

'But you're not—'

'I know, I know.'

Arguments circled wearily in Charlie's head. She could go on repeating the same points, but she saw that it wasn't simply a matter of standing up for Sean against Mr Fletcher, nor a matter of dismissing what onlookers thought. Sean's reputation could be called into question, whereas she would be seen as gullible victim. Sean was the teacher, the adult.

'Then how am I going to *see* you?' she appealed. 'I can't see you at home because of Mum, and now I can't see you anywhere else because of what people might think. Don't expect me to make do with the odd glimpse around school, because it's not enough. I miss you! I want to see you! You're my—' Her what? 'My *friend*.'

Sean looked at her without speaking. She wanted to cry. Everything about him was so familiar – the bones of his face, the set of his mouth, the way he stood with feet firmly planted and hands thrust deep into the pockets of his shorts. His muscular brown legs, with a scar on one knee where a dog had bitten him when he was eight. His way of tying the laces of his trainers in a double knot and bow. She thought of the card he'd written to her mother; imagined him in the florist's, writing it. The only answer was for him to marry Kathy, but that obviously wasn't going to happen.

'I don't know,' Sean said.

He was going to give her up, she thought. He wouldn't have time for her. Why should he, when her mother had rejected him over and over again? She saw the drab wastes of a Seanless future stretching into the distance, and felt a tug of misery deep in her chest. It came to her, suddenly and disturbingly, that she didn't want Sean to marry her mother, not any more. She didn't want him to marry anyone. She gazed at him hopelessly.

Then he said: 'I'll come and see you at Flightsend. Kathy will have to put up with it.'

A Midsummer Night's Dream was slick and funny. Charlie sat in the audience with Rowan and Russell and watched stern Theseus, resentful Helena and the other Athenians unfold their story, alternating with Peter Quince's bumbling crew, and ethereal Titania and her fairy entourage.

From Angus' first entrance as Oberon, Charlie saw that no one was going to make fun of him. There was nothing half-hearted or self-conscious about his performance. He strode on to the stage, swirled his cape, brooded jealously over Titania and her Indian boy and gave peremptory orders to Puck.

The play should have held Charlie's attention; she tried to enjoy herself, and to stop reliving the conversation with Sean. It was a clever, stylish production.

The cast had been well trained in covering up any errors they made, so that when Puck entered without his magical flower, one of the fairies clod-hopped on to the stage and presented it with a twirl to him and a curtsey to the audience, getting an unscheduled laugh.

Charlie felt weird. Almost sea-sick, she could have said. She didn't know quite when the ground had shifted, but it had, and now she was feeling her way in strange territory, sensing the unevenness, the tilting. It was no use pretending that she wanted Sean back for her mother's sake, nor even for his own. No use pretending that she wanted him as surrogate father or older brother.

She just wanted him.

She wanted him to want to be with her, and no one else.

She glanced at Rowan, who was whispering something to Russell, and thought: I can't tell anyone. Not Rowan. Not Mum. Least of all Sean himself. He mustn't know; it would spoil everything. Especially in the light of what he'd told her. If she wanted to go on seeing him, she mustn't give him anything to hide. In any case, he'd be horrified. And he still loved her mother; she had written evidence of that, from less than a week ago.

'*Wake when some vile thing is near . . .*'

When Charlie had been about twelve, old enough to take an interest in such things, she had asked both her mother and Sean, separately, about how they met, why they'd liked each other. She knew that their first real conversation, soon after Sean joined the school, had been at a staff social event, a meal at a restaurant. Sean, arriving late, had sat at the only spare seat, next to Kathy.

'I'd seen her at school and thought she was attractive,' Sean said, 'but it never occurred to me that we'd – you know – click like we did. She's older than me and she looked sophisticated, intelligent, and I knew she had a daughter so I just assumed there was a husband or partner as well. And there was me, the new boy, the clueless new teacher straight from college. Well, we started talking and we could have talked all night. Other people went home and the waitresses were clearing up around us and we were still there talking. We had about ten cups of coffee and then she gave me a lift home. Even so, it was ages before I had the guts to ask her out, and I thought she'd just laugh and brush me off. But I'm glad she didn't.'

Mum, asked about Sean, had said: 'I'd got him all wrong. Stereotyped him, really. I thought – young man, good-looking, sporty, athletic – he's bound to be arrogant. But he wasn't at all. I liked that.'

'What thou seest when thou dost wake, Do it for thy true love take . . .'

Sean and Mum. Mum and Sean. Charlie had thought they were a fixture. Sean's devotion to her mother was constantly expressed in hugs, touches, kisses; he was by far the more demonstrative of the two. Newly-curious about adult relationships, Charlie had learned to recognize the muffled sounds through the bedroom wall which meant that Sean and her mother were making love. Maybe she had even been listening when the baby was conceived. Rowan, currently engaged in a should-she/shouldn't-she dilemma about whether to go on the Pill, couldn't bear the thought of her parents having sex. 'I can't imagine it! I mean, my dad, with his beer gut! Do you think they actually still *do* it, at their age?' Charlie had known that her mother and Sean did, even before the pregnancy made it obvious; she didn't feel disgusted, like Rowan, only rather intrigued.

Now she thought: I'm in love with Sean. With my mother's ex-lover. She tried it out, hearing the way it sounded. No, to explain would be to cheapen it, turn it into a TV soap, a situation rife with conflict and dramatic potential. Alternatively, she was a teenage girl with a crush on a handsome teacher, like countless others who drew entwined initials on their pencil-cases, who batted their eyelids and flicked back their hair. That, too, reduced it to cliché. And what she felt wasn't just a crush, a temporary feeling for someone she hardly knew. She knew Sean better than anyone except her mother. They had walked up Lake District fells together; they had played tennis; she had brought him hot LemSip when he was ill with flu, and had waited at the hospital when he cracked a bone in his forearm. They'd made Mum's birthday cake together. He'd mended punctures on her bike and had gone with her on the sponsored ride for Oxfam. He and

Charlie had taken Conker to the vet to be put to sleep, and he'd cuddled Charlie when she cried afterwards. She knew his likes and dislikes, his favourite music, his moods. She knew his irritating habits, like leaving wet towels on the bathroom floor, and whistling the same tune over and over again while she was trying to do homework. Charlie and Mum would chorus, 'Oh, *Sean*,' but now she could only see these things as lovable. She wanted to be with him. Hear his voice. Have his attention.

'*Stay, though thou kill me, sweet Demetrius . . .*'

It felt wrong to be thinking of him in this new way. Almost incestuous. She thought: if Rose had lived, I wouldn't feel like this. *If.* Sean would be with Mum and everything would be simple. It's all Rose's fault.

She couldn't help it. She sat in the welcome semi-darkness, watching the play at one remove, lost in her thoughts.

'*What angel wakes me from my flowery bed?*'

Titania, bewitched by the magic juice, was falling in love with Bottom, who now wore a ridiculously hairy, floppy-eared donkey's head. Bottom was led off by bustling fairies; people were applauding, standing up, dropping their programmes, as the interval music began to play and the hall was flooded with light. Charlie stood blinking and dazed, suddenly faced with the need to make conversation, to say something about the play.

'Come on, Charlie, you don't look quite all there,' Russell said.

188

Rowan giggled. 'She's stage-struck. With Angus. He's brilliant, isn't he?'

She'd have to do better than this. Besides, the play deserved her full concentration. When the lights dimmed for the second half, she made herself pay attention. Angus would want her opinion, in detail.

The display of acting talent was formidable. All the main players were good, especially Pippa Woodford as Titania and a girl from year ten as a fiery Hermia, but Angus stood out. There was an expectant focus each time he came on stage; he could provoke laughter with the lift of an eyebrow.

'He looked good, too,' Rowan said in her father's car on the way home. 'Great costume, green tights and all. And that make-up. It made him look – not evil, but sort of dangerous.'

'Quite butch for a Fairy King.' Russell was next to her in the back seat, with Charlie in front. 'Pippa looked gorgeous, didn't she? And Hermia, in that clingy dress – what's that girl's name?'

'Hey! Eyes off!' Rowan warned, and her father said, 'I'm glad you found it such an educational experience, Russ. Never could get my head round Shakespeare when I was at school but it sounds like I should have come.'

Charlie said, 'Everything we saw – all those people, the costumes, the set – it happens once more tomorrow and then it's finished. All that effort, all that energy, and suddenly it's gone. If you weren't there, you missed it. They're taking the set down at the weekend, Angus said.'

'Someone was making a video,' Russell said. 'Those two blokes at the back. Didn't you see them?'

'But that's not the same at all,' Charlie said. 'And as soon as you watch it, it's in the past. That's what makes it a bit sad, really. I mean, never in their whole lives will all those people get together like that again.'

'They've had a great time doing it, though,' said Rowan's dad. 'Why be sorry because it can't go on for ever?'

Charlie thought of the last time she'd been given a lift home along these same country lanes. This time she had a great deal more confidence that she'd arrive home safely. It was a still, perfect summer evening, not quite dark; she saw the graceful shapes of trees above misted fields. Through the partly-open window she could smell cut grass, and see the mown hay laid out for drying. Suddenly she longed to be at home, alone.

'See you in a fortnight,' Rowan called as Charlie got out at the end of her lane. 'And we'll send you a post-card.'

'Have a great holiday! And thanks again for the lift,' Charlie said to Rowan's dad.

Kathy was reading in bed. Charlie went up, told her briefly about the play, then went down again and let herself and Caspar out into the garden.

She could smell the fresh dampness. In this still-not-darkness the white flowers gleamed as if floating in the dusk. She heard a fox bark and, in a field some way off, the baaing of sheep. The night air was cool, scented with grass and roses. Stirred up by the play and the midsummer night and the disturbing emotions that had got hold of her, she was reluctant to go indoors. She walked slowly down the path, touching the white phlox flowers, bending to breathe them in; at Frühlingsmorgen she stopped, and touched one of its fading blooms. She thought of Dietmar, and his arrival in their lives so unexpectedly − as if their discovery of his memorial rose had brought him here. If only the power of thought, or of wishing, could always be as effective. Quite what she wished for, she couldn't have said. Not long ago, if a midsummer fairy had appeared at the bottom of the garden and offered to grant one wish, she wouldn't have hesitated. I want everything back the way it was before, she'd have said. I want our old life back, with our old house, and Mum and Sean together. And the possibility of Rose, that wouldn't be snuffed out in the world of dream-wishes. But to wish for all that would be not to want Flightsend, or Caspar, and she wanted both those things.

'*Sean.*'

Caspar came bumbling up to her, leaning his weight against her legs and waving his tail wildly, turning his head to look at her. Only then did she realize she'd whispered the name aloud. Sean. She wanted everything, all ways at once. She wanted Sean as family and as not-family. She even wanted the ache that tugged at her now.

'Good boy. Let's go in.'

She gave Caspar a few biscuits, then went up to her room. She thought: you can't call the past back, and there's no point trying. You can only have it while it's present. Like the play tonight, it happens and then it's gone.

In the drawer where she kept her sweaters she had hidden the florist's card retrieved from the dustbin. She took it out, covering the top line of script with her thumb so that it read: *I love you. Sean.*

She felt ashamed of herself for pretending.

'Don't be so *stupid*,' she told herself. Then she put the card back in its place and got ready for bed.

Part Three

Scrapbook

'It was fantastic! Just amazing!'

Kathy was in her dressing-gown, putting croissants to warm in the oven. She'd come in late last night, having phoned to say that she and Dietmar, after their flight in the Cessna, had decided to go to a restaurant for dinner.

'That doesn't tell me much!' Charlie said. 'I want to hear all about it. Were you scared?'

'At first. It was so bumpy, on the runway, and the plane seemed so tiny and fragile, I thought it'd never get up into the sky. I was thinking, Why did I ever say I'd do this? And when it turned, it banked so suddenly that my stomach lurched. I was terrified, to be honest! And afraid of being sick. I mean, I've never liked flying in passenger jets, and in the Cessna it's so different – more obvious that you *are* flying. You're sitting in the sky in a tiny box with wings, buffeted about by the wind. But Dietmar was so good. All the time, he told me what he was doing and why, and he was so relaxed that I stopped shaking and started to enjoy myself.

And then I wasn't scared again till the landing, but that was all right, too. I don't know how long we were up, but it felt like hours – oh, it was wonderful, Charlie! We flew over Northampton and all the lakes and gravel-pits on the east side, and we saw Silverstone racetrack, and Stowe gardens with the avenues of trees – fantastic from the air. And we flew over here – did you see us?'

'No, I was reading in the garden for a while, but then I got engrossed and forgot to look.'

'We saw Flightsend, and the airfield, and the village – it looked so peaceful down here, with the church huddled into its trees, and the green, and all the fields spreading out – grass, and wheat, all soft hazy colours, and a combine harvester in one of the fields. Dietmar said he'll take you up next time, if you want to go.'

'Will he? Next time?' Charlie looked at her mother. 'So there's definitely a next time, is there?'

'Oh yes,' Kathy said promptly. 'I won't be so scared now I know what to expect.'

'I didn't mean that. I meant a next time for seeing Dietmar. But obviously there is.'

'Yes. I like him, Charlie. I like him a lot.' Kathy fetched the warm croissants and put them on the table with the butter and apricot jam. It was Monday, Charlie's day off from waitressing, although she was going round to look after Rosie this afternoon. On Nightingales breakfast mornings, there was barely time for a quick mug of tea together before Charlie got into her black skirt and rushed off. Monday breakfasts, more leisurely, had acquired special status.

'The dinner?' she prompted. 'How was that?'

'Oh, it was lovely. We went to a country hotel near the airfield. A quiet, elegant place, with a huge dining room overlooking a lake. I felt really scruffy, coming straight from the airfield, but it didn't matter. We just talked and talked.'

Charlie said nothing. She wished she could raise one eyebrow in enigmatic query, the way Angus could. *Talked and talked.* That was how it had started with Sean.

'Don't start thinking I'm about to marry him,' Kathy said, pouring coffee. 'I enjoy his company, that's all.'

'*All.* That's quite a big *all.* A big, important one.'

'Yes. Well. He's thoughtful, intelligent, kind – I know he's a lot older than me, nearly twenty years, but it doesn't matter.'

'Why should it?'

'You've changed your tune.' Kathy looked at Charlie, amused. 'You seemed horrified at first, when I told you about seeing Dietmar again.'

'Yes, but not because of his age! Because of—'

'Because of Sean?'

Charlie thought: she actually said his name. But Charlie didn't want to talk about Sean for fear of giving herself away.

'No,' she lied. 'Because I thought it might be dangerous, the flying. His *age* doesn't matter. Marianne ends up marrying Colonel Brandon and he's years older than her.' Charlie's English teacher, a Jane Austen addict, had suggested *Sense and Sensibility* for holiday reading; Charlie had just finished it, and she and her mother had watched the film.

'I can't quite see myself as Marianne,' her mother said. 'She's nearer your age than mine.'

'Mm.' Charlie hadn't really been thinking of her mother and Dietmar when she said that age didn't matter. What had struck her about *Sense and Sensibility* was that the age difference between Marianne and Colonel Brandon was bigger than the gap between Sean and herself.

'As for Kate Winslet in the film,' her mother continued, 'running over the moors in daft shoes – no wonder she sprained her ankle. Anyway, she may have married Colonel Brandon but that doesn't mean I'm going to marry Dietmar or anyone else. Unlike Marianne, I've tried it once and I've no great desire to try again.'

Charlie saw that there *was* a parallel between Marianne and Mum. OK, Marianne was much younger, but had found happiness with Colonel Brandon after having a breakdown and becoming seriously ill when her first love affair ended. That part fitted, anyway, sort of. The rest didn't. It was handsome, dashing Willoughby who'd broken off with Marianne, not the other way round. Charlie had thought Willoughby was too good to be true, right from the start, especially in the film. Marianne was the loyal, faithful one, even if she loved the wrong person. Charlie was reading *Emma* now, and was about to suggest getting the film of that, but her mother wasn't going to be distracted from the topic of Dietmar.

'I thought I'd invite him for lunch next Sunday. You don't mind, do you?'

'No,' Charlie said. It came out on a doubtful note.

'Dietmar's a friend. A good friend. At the moment, that's all I want. Him being so much older is fine. He's mature, in charge of his life. He's been married, he's got grown-up children. He doesn't make demands. He's happy the way things are.'

'So that's OK,' Charlie said flippantly.

She didn't like the implication that Sean had been unreasonably demanding, wanting to stay when everything went wrong. But she wasn't going to argue today.

'Did he ever tell you why he left Flightsend, when he liked it so much?' she asked.

'He was lonely,' Kathy said. 'He'd always lived in a city till he came here. He bought Flightsend just after his wife left him. But he realized it was a mistake to bury himself in the depths of the country, when he wasn't used to it.'

'Why did she leave?' Charlie asked.

Kathy looked at her. 'She left him for a much younger man.'

It was August now, the summer holidays proper. Sean was away in North Wales; Rowan, back from Tenerife, was spending a few days with Russell and his Scottish grandparents. Dietmar had been visiting family in Germany since the week after the fête, which was why the Cessna flight had waited till now. It was the time of year when normal life was on pause.

Charlie missed Sean so badly that she felt ill. Sick, dizzy, floaty, like having a high temperature. She walked the footpaths with Caspar, she studied the map and found new routes. She walked down by the river, where the water slid darkly beneath overhanging trees, between banks lush with reed and willowherb. *Sean, Sean.* His name throbbed in her head like a pulse; it was in the rustle of leaves and the stillness of the river and the whisper of her feet brushing through grasses.

All the time, she stored things up in her mind to tell him. Ordinary, everyday things; things to make him laugh. She wasn't going to tell him how completely he occupied her thoughts. They'd met once since the end of term, just before he went away. He'd kept his promise and had taken her and Caspar up to Dovedale, in the Peak District. They had walked and clambered over rocks and eaten a picnic, and Sean started teaching her how to navigate with a map and compass. Charlie knew that people who passed them saw a young man and a girl, boyfriend and girlfriend, out for the day together. She could pretend.

She kept replaying the day in her mind, holding on to it.

She tried to draw him. Never before had she drawn a portrait without the person sitting in front of her; it was impossibly difficult. When she closed her eyes she could see Sean quite clearly, could visualize a whole range of his expressions; but when she tried to commit any one of them to paper, Sean disappeared and was replaced by a set of features that bore no resemblance to his. She tried to draw him from the Great Gable photograph, but that was too small and blurry. What came from her pencil was a smiling face that could have been anyone's.

Oliver Locke was staying in the Well House while he completed the sketches for the Nightingales brochure, and was running courses most weekends. That afternoon, when Charlie arrived, he was carrying a box of groceries into the store room. He told her about his Watercolour group at the weekend, and asked if she'd like to join in. Charlie thought she would. At school they always used acrylics, and she liked the delicacy of watercolours.

'Aren't you going on holiday?' she asked him. 'It doesn't seem much of a break for you, all these courses.'

'Can't afford it this year,' he told her. 'I've got a lot of big expenses coming up. Next year, when I'm settled, I'll go to Tuscany. Anyway, I like it here.'

Charlie collected Rosie, and took her down to feed the ducks; afterwards they settled in the courtyard, sitting together on the bench with Rosie's picture-book.

'There's Wosie,' Rosie said, prodding a damp forefinger.

And then Charlie jumped as a shadow fell across the book and a warm hand cupped her shoulder. Oliver, again.

Rosie was delighted. 'Orriver! Orriver! We're having a story!'

For the first time, Charlie felt a tremor of irritation. He liked to do that, she realized; sneak up on her, surprise her. How long had he been there? She felt embarrassed at the thought of him listening while she talked to Rosie about the pictures in *Rosie's Walk*.

'You know,' he said abruptly, 'it looked so picturesque when I came along. The two of you, absorbed in the book. The sunlight on your hair. Like a sentimental Victorian painting.'

Charlie looked at him, puzzled at his tone. It was faintly sarcastic – his choice of words, *picturesque*, *sentimental*; but there was something else. Sadness? Envy?

There wasn't room for him on the bench, where Rosie sat next to Charlie with her legs spread out. He sat on the arm, close to Charlie. A little too close. She moved nearer to Rosie.

'I've seen your mother here a couple of times,' he said. 'Talking to Fay about the garden plans. You know when you mentioned your mum, and Sean Freeland – you didn't tell me about the baby. I'm sorry.'

'Who *did* tell you?' Charlie said sharply. 'Not Mum, surely?'

'No, it was Fay. She and your mum seem to be getting quite friendly.'

They must be, Charlie thought, if Mum had talked about Rose; usually she kept the subject tightly zipped up inside. And to *Fay*, of all people, with Rosie around . . . perhaps Rosie's presence had been the prompt. But Charlie didn't like the idea of her mother being gossiped about at Nightingales.

'*Fox*,' Rosie said, stabbing a finger at the picture. Clumsily, she turned a page.

'That's right, Rosie,' Charlie said. She returned her attention to the story, but Oliver spoke again.

'It must have been tough for you, as well as for Kathy,' he said. 'So all this—' he waved an arm at Rosie, the bench, the book – 'is sort of therapy?'

'For me, you mean? I don't know. I mean, it just happened. Fay asked me, and I said yes.'

'You like coming here, don't you? As much as I do.' Oliver bent to pick up her sketchbook from the ground, and started to leaf through the pages. 'And these?' He'd found the sketches of Rosie. 'Therapy?'

It had become a habit for Charlie to show him her drawings, but this time she hadn't offered them. These weren't for him. Charlie watched him in silence. Rosie said, 'Tarm-yard.'

Oliver studied the drawings carefully, turned the pages. 'These are nice – these quick little line draw-ings. Catching the pose.'

'It's difficult, like you told me,' Charlie said.

'Mmm, I can see.'

'I was having a go at drawing in pen. I like it. You can't fiddle about like you can with pencil.'

He continued looking. Too late, she realized that he'd turned the page to her ineffectual sketches of Sean. She went to snatch the book back, but he smiled at what he saw, then said, 'You must let me return the compliment, some time soon. I'd love to draw you. Paint you, even better.'

Was there something suggestive about the way his gaze swept down her body? And he thought—

'No. No,' she said, her cheeks burning. She didn't want to explain that the drawings were of Sean, not of him. Fortunately they were too bad for him to tell. She tugged at the sketchbook and turned back to the Rosie sketches. He liked to think she spent her time dreaming about him; she saw that now.

He looked amused at her embarrassment. 'The pen drawings are much better,' he said, as if she didn't know. Then, 'You look after Rosie quite a lot now, don't you? D'you think you might look after Kieran for me, this Friday afternoon?'

'Kieran?'

'My son.'

She didn't know he had a son. They'd talked quite often, but he'd never mentioned Kieran.

'Nice name. How old is he?'

'Seven.'

'It's a bit different from looking after Rosie.'

'Not an awful lot,' said Oliver, 'He's no real trouble.'

'Does he live with his mother?'

'Yes.'

'Don't you see him much?'

204

Was this the reason for his reticence? The failure of his marriage, separation from his son? He rarely mentioned his ex-wife. Another relationship ended, Charlie thought. What's wrong with everyone?

'Not very often,' he said. 'It's difficult.'

'Is he staying the whole weekend?'

'No, I'm just having him on Friday. Rosalind's got an appointment and her usual child-minder can't have him. But I need to sit down with Fay and Dan and go through next year's programme. So if you could keep an eye on him, just for an hour or two . . .'

'OK, then,' she said. It could be a repayment for all the free tuition; besides, she was curious to see Kieran.

'Thanks, Charlie. I appreciate it.'

He touched her arm, and let his hand rest there for a moment. She was uneasy about the way he kept touching her; a pat on the shoulder, a hand on her waist to guide her, his hand over hers while she was drawing. At first, flattered by his interest, she'd taken it for friendliness. Now, especially since the conversation with Sean, she knew he shouldn't do it. He was assuming some sort of right over her. She thought of saying, 'Please don't touch me,' but saw at once how he'd take it. He was only being friendly, affectionate; she'd be neurotic, even conceited, to imagine she was so desirable that he couldn't keep his hands off her.

But no one should touch her if she didn't want them to.

It would be easy enough to be assertive if the person

doing the touching were a stranger, or someone drunk at a party, but the grey areas were more difficult. When you knew – even liked – the person, or when the gestures might express nothing more than friendliness or reassurance, it was impossible to shout, or be aggressive. Even more difficult when you weren't sure whether you liked it or not.

Was she making too much of it? Probably. She didn't seriously imagine he was planning a steamy affair, to be conducted in the Well House between workshops. He was a teacher and she was a schoolgirl.

'Right. Friday, then,' she said abruptly. 'Come on, Rosie. Let's go indoors.'

'What have you been drawing lately?' Kathy asked, that evening.

An impulse made Charlie push her sketchbook across the table.

'These. Have a look.'

At once she wanted to take it back.

Kathy got no farther than the sketches of Rosie. Saying nothing, she looked at each one, then turned back to the most detailed portrait, the one Charlie had finished at home. The one that didn't really look like Rosie.

Finally she said, 'You know who she makes me think of?'

'No.' Charlie dreaded the answer. *She looks like Rose. Rose as she would have been.* That's what Kathy would say. What had possessed her to hand over the drawings?

She'd have done better to tear them into shreds.

'She looks like you. When you were that age,' Kathy said. 'Thank you for showing me.'

She closed the sketchbook and went upstairs.

Charlie, who'd expected tears, reproaches, even anger, stood uncertainly at the bottom of the stairs. She waited to hear the bedroom door closing, but instead she heard Kathy rummaging about in cupboards. A few minutes later she came down again, carrying a cardboard box.

'What have you got there?'

'Photos,' Kathy said.

She dumped the box on the kitchen table and tilted it towards Charlie. Inside, Charlie saw two large scrapbooks, and dozens of photographs – some loose, most still as they came from processing, in their paper wallets.

'I should have sorted these out years ago, and put them in the scrapbook,' her mother said. 'Do you want to help?'

It took them until half-past one in the morning. Sorting, identifying, writing captions. Some of the photographs went into the scrapbook; others stayed in their wallets, labelled and dated.

Most of the pictures that went into the scrapbook were of Charlie. Charlie as a baby, with her father – a strange, remote figure he seemed now, as distant as someone in a Victorian aquatint. Charlie at about three, sitting on a pony with Kathy supporting her.

Charlie in the nativity play at her infant school, a sturdy, scowling angel with wonky tinsel wings.

'I love this one,' her mother said, holding up the one of Charlie on the pony. 'We stayed on a farm in Devon, just you and me. The pony was called Bumble and you wanted to bring her home. Do you remember?'

'Very vaguely.'

Charlie reached out for the photo, but her mother held on to it.

'I'll see if I can find the negative. I'll get it enlarged and framed.'

Charlie was assistant, letting her mother do it her own way; she sorted and glued and labelled according to instructions. It was more than the carrying-out of a job long overdue; it was a journey into their past. When Sean began to appear in the pictures Kathy made no particular comment, other than to identify the time and place where she could. Charlie wrote captions, looked briefly, said little. Now that she knew where the photos were, she could find them again later.

'Me pregnant,' her mother said, matter-of-factly, passing over a print.

Charlie didn't know how much that casual tone could be trusted. Sorting the photographs had put her mother in a strange mood: nostalgic, a little sad, but with a sort of hypnotized calm.

'You should have been in bed long ago,' Kathy said, when Charlie had stuck in the most recent pictures –

those of Flightsend, mainly of the nursery at various stages of development, and one or two of Caspar. 'I hope you won't be worn out tomorrow. Thank you. That was a good thing to do.' She kissed Charlie and picked up the box.

Lying in bed and contemplating the strange evening, Charlie thought about the word *scrapbook*. The books of photos weren't really scrapbooks but albums; a real scrapbook would contain things other than photos – letters, tickets, programmes, wrappers. But the word stuck in her mind. Scraps. Scraps of their lives. Scraps that could have been discarded, but hadn't been.

Kieran

Fridays were always busy at Nightingales, with one lot of guests leaving after lunch and a second batch arriving for dinner. In today's changeover, Creative Collage and Feng Shui gave way to Watercolour Painting and Be More Assertive.

'We'll easily tell who's here for Assertiveness,' Jon said at breakfast-time. 'It'll be the ones who look meek and helpless when they arrive.'

'And get more and more bolshy as the weekend goes on,' Suzanne added. 'Expect trouble with the orders by Sunday lunchtime.'

Charlie, having arranged to look after Rosie and Kieran from three o'clock till just before dinner, wore jeans and the batik top from Henrietta's, bringing her waitressing clothes and shoes in a carrier bag. She found Fay in the office and collected Rosie. Having seen no sign of Oliver, she went over to the Well House to see if he was there.

'Orriver! Orriver!' Rosie ran ahead towards the open door, arms flailing.

'Hello there, Rosie Rascal.' Oliver appeared from inside, picking Rosie up and lifting her high above his head. She squealed and wriggled until he put her down. Then he said, 'Hi, Charlie. Kieran's in here.'

A large, thick-set boy was sitting on the floor. He looked round slowly as Charlie entered. She saw the slackness of his mouth, the rather prominent eyes, slow to focus; the clumsy movement as he struggled to his feet. His arms and legs were short in proportion to his body. It was like looking at a younger version of Oliver that had become blurred and distorted.

'This is Kieran,' Oliver said.

Kieran stared at Charlie, his mouth open. She thought: Down's Syndrome? Why didn't Oliver tell me?

'Hello, Kieran,' she said; then Rosie went up and took him by the hand.

'Tieran, Tieran! Tieran come with us.'

'They know each other?' Charlie asked Oliver, who stood back watching.

'Oh yes,' he said. 'They've played together quite often. You see what I mean, about it not being much different from looking after Rosie.'

'What does he like to do?' she asked. 'What would you like to do, Kieran? Come and feed the ducks?'

'Yeah, go and feed the ducks,' Oliver said. 'You needn't bother too much. He's usually quite happy to sit and stare.'

'I'll think of something,' Charlie told him. 'Right, I'll see you back here at half-past five.'

'Have fun,' he said. 'If he needs the loo, bring him up to the office. I'll have to take him.' He locked the Well House behind them and walked off towards the house.

Charlie, with her two charges, went down the sloping lawn to the pond, one hand holding Kieran's, one holding Rosie's. Rosie clutched the bag of stale bread; Kieran stumbled on the uneven ground, and Charlie adjusted her pace. Adjusted her thoughts, too. Was this why Oliver never mentioned Kieran? Was he ashamed of him?

'Kook,' Rosie said, pointing, as a coot bobbed out from behind the reeds.

'*Coot*, Rosie.'

'Toot.'

By now Charlie was sure that Rosie knew the difference between *t* and *c*, but liked muddling them up for fun. She handed pieces of bread to both children. Rosie, with cries of excitement, aimed hers at the indifferent coot. Kieran tore his up with slow deliberation, then stepped close to the water's edge and flung a piece of crust hard but ineptly, so that it landed in the shallows near his feet. He crouched to dabble with his hand, waiting for the soggy bread to float close enough to catch. Charlie watched, slightly anxious in case he fell in; he'd be a heavy boy to pull out of the water. But his feet were firmly planted, and when the bread was dripping in his hand he stepped back from the edge.

Charlie hadn't yet heard him speak. She wondered

if he *did* speak. Then Rosie came up and tried to take the wet crust from him, and Kieran made a sound of objection, turning away.

'It's yours, isn't it, Kieran?' Charlie said, restraining Rosie. 'Rosie's got her own.'

The mallards had been slow to arrive but now they clustered round with expectant quackings. One of the bolder ones clambered out to the bank, waddled up to Rosie and tugged at the hem of her skirt. Kieran, perhaps thinking the duck was attacking Rosie, flapped his arms to shoo it away. 'Nnno! Nnno!'

'Well done, Kieran,' Charlie said.

He looked at her and said, 'Woshor name?' His voice was thick and nasal, the words slurred.

'My name's Charlie,' she said, pronouncing it clearly. Oliver hadn't actually introduced her to Kieran. Kieran had simply come with her, obedient and unquestioning. Maybe he was used to a variety of carers.

'Charlie,' Kieran repeated. He stared at her, his head swaying a little. Then he said, 'Boy.'

'That's right, it *is* a boy's name,' she said. 'But it's a girl's name too. Short for Charlotte.'

'Tarlotte,' Rosie said. 'Rosie, Wosary.'

Charlie laughed. '*Rosemary*? Is that your name, Rosie?'

'Wosary,' Rosie insisted.

When all the bread was gone the mallards dispersed, some settling on the bank to preen, some dabbling tail-up in the water. As the children showed

213

no signs of boredom, Charlie sat on the grass to watch them. Rosie was absorbed in prodding the damp grass with a stick; Kieran went down to the water's edge and collected five rounded stones, which he placed carefully in the palm of one hand. Then he brought them close to Charlie and laid them on the grass. When he'd done this three times, Rosie became interested. Wanting to play too, she brought a collection of pebbles and presented them to Kieran.

Kieran lowered himself heavily to the grass and began to arrange his stones in a pattern. Charlie saw that he'd chosen a particular kind of stone, rejecting most of Rosie's; he wanted the smooth, rounded rust-coloured ones, fairly uniform in size. He put each stone down very carefully and patted it into place with the flat of his hand, breathing hard. Charlie watched; Rosie copied, bringing more and more stones and making her own arrangement. Rosie's was straight lines with occasional heaps, like little cairns to mark a path; Kieran was making a spiral shape.

When she took the children up to the kitchen for orange juice and biscuits, Jon made her a cup of tea and said, 'I feel sorry for that kid, poor little sod.'

'Oh?' Charlie was trying not to take her eyes off Rosie. Kieran, she had found, would wait where he was put, like a dog told to sit and stay; Rosie was likely to knock something over or dash too near the hobs, where Jon had two large casseroles steaming.

'He's always being dumped on someone,' Jon said. 'Last year it was Francesca.'

'Francesca?'

'Oh, I forgot – you weren't here then,' Jon said. 'She was Oliver's girlfriend – no one was meant to know, but I used to see her sneaking out of the Well House in the mornings. Oliver doesn't bring the kid here much now. His wife – ex-wife – has him most of the time.'

Charlie's thoughts had snagged on the name *Francesca*. Francesca Abbott. Oliver's star student.

'What did she look like?' she asked casually. 'Francesca?'

Jon lifted a lid, dipped a spoon and tasted, then fetched a pepper-grinder and twisted vigorously. 'Oh – quite striking. Tall. Thin. Cropped hair. Stylish, in a way all her own. She wore clothes that looked like cut-up curtains and bedspreads.'

That was Francesca Abbott, unmistakably. Charlie remembered Lisa, in the art corridor, saying, 'She's *this* year's teacher's pet. You're next.'

Uneasiness curdled in Charlie's stomach. She showed nothing, sipping her tea, watching Kieran and Rosie. She'd laughed at what Lisa said, but it was true.

Oliver and Francesca. Not just touching. Sleeping together.

And now? Was Oliver cultivating her as Francesca's replacement?

Could Jon have got it wrong? There was nothing objectionable about Francesca being here, or looking after Kieran. But staying in the Well House! If there was an innocent reason for that, Charlie couldn't think of one. Surely Dan and Fay wouldn't condone it. But if they didn't *know* . . .

Charlie's brain was on full spin. She didn't know what she thought. She tried to shove Oliver out of her head, and to concentrate on the children.

When Kieran and Rosie had finished their drinks, she took them to the courtyard, with the picture-book Fay had left for them in the hall. They sat on the bench, squashed together three in a row, the book on Charlie's lap. As usual, Rosie was eager for the story to continue, trying to prise the corner of the page from under Charlie's fingers. Kieran sat passively, his lips moving to some sound in his own head, not to the words Charlie was reading.

Then, half-way through the story, he said loudly, 'Nay.'

'Nay?'

'Nay. Nail.'

Charlie looked at him, then at the double-page spread, for some clue.

'Snay.' He pointed at the garden wall.

Then Charlie understood. 'Snail!' There was a tiny snail as the footer to each page, making its way across the book on a trail of slime, so that if you flicked through the pages it appeared to be moving. She did this to show Kieran and Rosie.

'Snay.' He pointed again. Charlie looked, but saw no snail on the wall. 'See snay.'

It was Rosie who got it. 'Snail. Tieran maked a snail.'

'A snail of stones! You made a snail, Kieran? Shall we go back and see it?'

Kieran nodded vigorously. There was a trail of dribble from his mouth to his chin; Charlie wiped it away with a tissue. For the second time they all went down to the pond, Kieran stumbling in his haste, talking to himself.

'Snail, yes. I can see now. Clever Kieran!' Charlie said, by the pattern of stones.

Rosie began to make a snail of her own, while Kieran made adjustments to his. Charlie was in no hurry to take them away; she didn't know how she'd face Oliver. Soon the new guests would arrive, exclaiming as they saw the pond, coming down to look; but for now there was only the *prukk* of a coot and the flick and splash as a fish broke the surface. The water mirrored sky between the cut-out shapes of waterlily leaves. While the harvested fields beyond were taking on the bleached look of late summer, the pond and its banks were still green and luxuriant.

Charlie's thoughts kept circling round Oliver. She resisted, thinking instead of Sean, and the postcard he'd sent from Snowdonia. Sent it to *her*, not to Kathy. First to the doormat, she'd snatched it up, her instinct to hide it; but then she decided to show it to her mother. It was a test for both of them: for Kathy, to see if she could respond with normal interest; for Charlie, whether she could mention Sean's name without giving herself away.

'Look, Mum,' she said casually. 'A postcard from Sean.'

'Oh, yes?'

The moment passed without a display of emotion from either party.

Snowdon, Crib Goch was the picture: a terrifying ridge knifing the sky. Sean had written *Came across here today. A few hairy moments! Fantastic views – you'd love it. The course is tough, but by now I could navigate my way to any rock you care to name, in thick fog at midnight. See you soon, Sean.* Followed by an *x*.

Already Charlie knew the words by heart.

How soon? she wanted to ask him. When will I see you?

She would tell him about Kieran; she heard herself telling him. About Mum and the photos? About *Oliver*? She wasn't sure, but she imagined him sitting beside her, listening. She could visualize him so strongly that his absence was a fresh disappointment.

She'd forgotten the time, here in the still hollow of afternoon.

Someone was calling her.

'Charlie?' It was Oliver, walking quickly down the grass slope. 'What are you doing down here? It's gone half-past!'

'Oh, sorry.'

'I've got to get Kieran back to Rosalind for six. Anyway, sorry to lumber you. I hope he was OK.'

'I wasn't lumbered! I enjoyed it. Look at the snail Kieran's made—'

She moved towards it, but Oliver gave the briefest of glances and said, 'Oh, he's always playing about with stones. Come on, Kieran. We're going.'

He's always being dumped on someone, Jon had said, about Kieran. Oliver thought of him as a nuisance.

He didn't see him often; he'd told Charlie that. Naïvely, she had imagined a custody dispute, with Oliver frustrated in his desire to spend more time with his son. The real situation showed him in a far less flattering light. He was in charge of Kieran for one afternoon, but couldn't be bothered. Had palmed him off on someone else.

Kieran deserved better. Charlie felt a flash of loyalty towards him. And of hot, angry resentment towards Oliver.

Kieran walked slowly towards them. Waiting, Oliver said, 'Thanks again, Charlie. You've helped me out of a hole.' He smiled at her, reached a hand to touch her sleeve. 'This colour's fantastic on you. You ought to wear green more often.'

Charlie snatched her arm away and glared, taking three steps back. He met her gaze, puzzled and half-smiling. She moved towards Kieran. 'I've enjoyed our afternoon,' she told him. 'Thank you, Kieran.'

'Eye-bye arr,' he said. Charlie saw the slow beginning of a smile.

'I'll be back for dinner and to meet the troops,' Oliver told her, 'and then I'll see you tomorrow for the class.'

'No, you won't,' Charlie said. 'I'm not coming.'

'Oh?' Oliver looked a question at her, but then glanced at his watch. 'God, look at the time. Come *on*, Kieran. See you when I get back, Charlie.'

Kieran turned to wave to Rosie. Oliver started up the slope without him, then turned and waited; before Kieran had caught up, he walked on again. Charlie noticed that for all the touching Oliver did, he hadn't touched Kieran once: no hug for a greeting, no physical sign of affection at all. He'd barely spoken to him, and then impatiently. He hadn't asked whether he'd had a nice time, or admired the snail, or explained why it was time to go. He treated Kieran as an unwieldy piece of baggage.

Charlie watched them walking, together but apart.

She rarely thought about her own father, but now she did.

Her father had abandoned her. Didn't want her, didn't care. Money arrived in her mother's bank account each month but there was never a letter, never a phone call. He had no curiosity about her. She'd grown up, become a person; but not to him. He'd forgotten her.

She looked at Oliver's back as he walked up the lawn, and thought: *I hate you.*

But no, she didn't. Didn't care enough to hate him. She despised him.

Oliver Locke had less time for his own son than he had for her. And for Francesca. She remembered him saying he liked the Well House because of its distance from the guests; that wasn't just for artistic isolation, as she'd once liked to think. Had there been others before Francesca? How had he got away with it?

Not any more, she thought. Not if he thinks I'm going to play.

'Come on, Rosie,' she said. 'Time to find your mum.'

Coming in, late, at the front gate of Flightsend, Charlie almost tripped over four full dustbin bags left outside. They were black, easy to fall over in the near-darkness. Her mother had been having a clear-out.

The downstairs lights were still on. Kathy was sitting at the table reading a rose catalogue.

'Hi, Mum. What's in those bags?' Charlie asked, fending off Caspar.

'Baby things,' Kathy said. 'I decided there's no point hanging on to them any more. Someone put a flier through the letterbox – there's a Salvation Army collection tomorrow.'

'What – *all* of them?'

'I kept a little pair of shoes and a toy panda. Everything else is in the bags. It's silly to clutter up the loft when someone else can use the things.'

Well. Charlie didn't know what to say. Resisting an urge to rush out and haul the bags back indoors, she filled the kettle, making an unnecessary clatter with the mugs and milk jug. Somehow, she'd provoked this by showing her mother the drawings of Rosie.

'I was looking at Frühlingsmorgen this evening,' Kathy said. 'And thinking that we ought to plant a memorial rose of our own. A rose for Rose. You can help me choose. We'll go to a specialist rose grower to make sure we get exactly the one we want.'

'Yes. Good idea. Plant it here in the garden, you mean? We'll stay here now, won't we?'

'I think so,' Kathy said. 'This is home now, isn't it? I don't want anything else.'

Charlie looked at the kitchen shelf where she'd propped Sean's postcard. She thought: if this is some kind of final farewell, a putting to rest, he ought to be involved, too.

'Mum, I—' she began.

'Mmm?' Kathy looked up from the catalogue.

'Oh – I – think it's a really good idea, the rose,' Charlie said lamely.

She poured the tea and took hers up to bed. Picking up *Emma*, she stared at a page sightlessly, thinking that Sean would be at home now. For how long? He'd told her that he was setting straight off again, for Turkey. He was going on the cheap, he said, staying at Youth Hostels wherever he could. That way he could stay for three weeks. *Three weeks* – an interminable, unbearable stretch of time. Charlie felt as if she'd never see him again.

She was too hot. She threw back her quilt, opened the window wider, tried again to read. No use. A moth blundered against the lamp with a dry flicker of wings. She turned off the lamp to usher it out of the window, then stood for a while thinking. Sean was at home now, at the other end of a telephone, not miles away and inaccessible in Snowdonia or Turkey.

What would she say?

She couldn't phone now. Eleven at night was too late to bother him.

She didn't know what to do. If she had felt ill before, it was more like a fever now; she'd never sleep tonight. She fidgeted, picked things up, put them down again. What had Anne called her? Sensible, mature? She ought to see me now, she thought. Anyway, I don't want to be sensible and mature all the time. I'm only sixteen and I want to behave like a headstrong teenager for once. I've been sensible and mature for Mum; at least, I've tried to be. Now I want something for myself.

I want Sean.

I've got to talk to him. *Now*. Or go mad.

She heard bathroom sounds; her mother was getting ready for bed. When the buzz of the shower clicked on, Charlie crept down to the phone and dialled Sean's number.

He picked up almost straight away. 'Sean Freeland.'

So easy. His voice in her ear, warm and close.

'Sean, it's me.' Charlie tried to sound normal.

'Hi there, Charleston! How's things?'

'Fine, thanks. I'm sorry to phone so late. I just wanted' – *what?* – 'to see if you got home all right. I mean, anything could have happened. You could have fallen off Crib Goch. It looked terrifying.'

'Not this time, thanks. I held on tight.'

'You weren't asleep, were you? I hope you don't mind me phoning so late. I've missed you.'

'Course I don't mind! No, I was just about to turn in. I haven't been in long. Look, I was going to come over tomorrow afternoon. Would that be OK? I'll tell you all about it then.'

'You're coming here?'

'You don't have to sound so amazed. I won't get lost, not after a whole week with map and compass.'

'I thought you were going straight off to Turkey?'

'Not till Monday,' Sean said.

Charlie bounded upstairs two at a time and into bed. *Tomorrow!* Not three weeks ahead, not some time in an unforeseeable future, but *tomorrow*. He needn't come, he could find any number of reasons not to – too tired, washing and packing to do, other people to see – but he was coming here to see her. To see *her*.

She opened *Emma*. Chapter 47. Newly energized and not at all sleepy, she thought she might finish the book tonight.

She read: *It darted through her, with the speed of an arrow, that Mr Knightley must marry no one but herself!*

Mr Knightley. Sixteen years older than Emma. Someone Emma had regarded as a sort of older brother, or uncle, before realizing that she loved him.

Sean was thirteen years older than Charlie. Not sixteen. Not as old as Mr Knightley.

Admittedly, Mr Knightley hadn't been the lover of Emma's mother; not Jane Austen territory. All the same, the similarities were there. Now she had to know how *Emma* ended. Reading much too quickly, devouring the words, she read to Chapter 49, where Mr Knightley returned after an absence; Emma had been longing to see him – yes, yes, he loved her, he was telling her, they were clearing up all their misunderstandings. By Chapter 50 Emma was in 'a flutter of happiness'.

Charlie turned off her lamp, thinking of tomorrow, wondering what she was expecting. Not Emma's happy flutter; she didn't want any drastic change in the relationship. Didn't want to spoil it. Didn't even want Sean to touch her, other than to give his normal hug. Caressing or kissing would be too creepily Oliver Locke-like, crossing barriers that couldn't be crossed yet. To Sean, she was Charleston, good old Charleston. She was happy to go on being Charleston if it meant Sean was her friend, if he sent postcards and made time to be with her.

He loved her; she knew he did. Not in the dizzy, sick-with-longing way she now loved him; but still. It was more than enough to make her happy.

Flight's End

When the guests came in for Sunday breakfast, Charlie sneaked a look round the doorway to see where Oliver Locke was sitting.

'You do this end, I'll do the other,' she said to Suzanne.

'OK. You get the newly-assertive. Don't give them burnt toast or slopped coffee.'

Charlie had successfully avoided Oliver all weekend. He'd tried to talk to her on Friday night, cornering her in the entrance hall: 'Look, I'm sorry if you didn't like having Kieran. I won't ask you again.'

He was so thick-skinned; he didn't understand at all. Aloof, Charlie told him, 'I liked having Kieran. He's great. I don't mind having him again.' It's *you* I've taken a dislike to, she added silently, moving off with her tray of glasses before he could say more. At each meal-time since, she'd made sure Suzanne did the waitressing for his end of the table. ('What, did he pinch your bum, or something?' Suzanne asked. 'I'm still waiting for him to pinch mine.') Charlie didn't want to see more of Oliver than she had to; but at dinner she noticed that he'd seated himself next to the youngest and most attractive woman on his course, and was giving her the full dazzle of attentiveness and charm.

When the breakfast tables had been cleared and the dishwashers stacked, Charlie had toast and coffee with Jon and Suzanne before leaving for home. Oliver and his group had set up their easels on the lawn. It would have been good to learn water-colour technique, but she no longer wanted Oliver to be the one to teach her. She felt ashamed of her recent wish to produce something that would win his praise. Until she went back to school, she'd work for her own approval, no one else's. There were always two groups of students for sixth-form Art; she'd ask to be in Ms Pearson's class rather than Oliver's.

Today Dietmar was coming for lunch. Charlie couldn't remember when her mother had last cooked for a visitor, other than Anne; when Charlie left she'd been in the full fluster of preparation. As she'd be back at Nightingales at lunchtime, Charlie thought she'd leave her mother to it, and take Caspar out.

In a few hours' time, she'd see Sean.

Perhaps it wasn't a good idea for Sean to come at the same time as Dietmar. Last night, overwhelmed by the thought of seeing him at all, she'd forgotten that small detail. Perhaps Mum and Dietmar would go out after lunch . . .

She rounded the bend towards the village green

and there Sean was, walking towards her.

Charlie stopped. She had conjured him so often into her thoughts that she almost thought he was a mirage. This *afternoon*, he'd said.

He smiled, waved, came up to her. 'Are you OK, Charleston? You look like you've seen a ghost.'

'I'm fine,' she said, her words muffled into his shoulder as he hugged her. He smelled freshly-showered, of mint shampoo and something astringent. Just for a second she let herself imagine it was a real, romantic embrace.

'Kathy said I'd find you at Nightingales,' he said. 'She was frantically chopping and weighing things.'

'She's got someone coming for lunch.'

'Yes, she told me. The German guy.'

'Oh,' Charlie said uneasily. 'I hope she wasn't – you know, rude or anything? You know how she can be. I thought you said this afternoon?'

'Yes, I did, but then the bloke in the flat downstairs asked if I'd help unload a piano this afternoon, so I'm here now. And no, Kathy was all right. She even made me coffee while I waited, because she said you'd be busy. She said why don't I get you to show me round Nightingales.'

'OK. Let's go back there. You haven't got long, though, if you're sorting yourself out for Turkey *and* heaving pianos. Actually *I* haven't got long.' She looked at her watch. 'We start getting ready for lunch at half-past eleven.'

'Better than nothing. I'd like to see Nightingales,

anyway, after hearing so much about it.'

Having spent all week in imaginary conversation with Sean, Charlie couldn't now remember a single thing she'd wanted to say. She walked beside him, trying to fix every detail in her mind to be taken out later, and treasured. His feet, in black laced boots, walking beside hers. His sideways look and smile; the exact green-brown of his eyes. The husky note in his voice when he laughed.

He told her about his week in Wales, about the Crib Goch climb and the micro-navigation, by which time they were in the grounds of Nightingales, outside the dining-room window. Kathy's garden design was beginning to take shape. Builders had been in to lay the paths and to make the raised pond on the terrace, and soon Kathy would start the planting.

'It's all bare and new at the moment,' Charlie said, 'but if you imagine it with shrubs and plants, it'll look really good. Mum's shown me the drawings.'

Sean looked round at the mullioned windows and the rampant wisteria. 'It'll suit the house. She ought to do more of this. She's good at it.'

'Yes, I think she will, now. This was a good start, because lots of people will see it. Fay said Mum ought to put an advert in the entrance hall. She even wants Mum to be a course tutor. I think Mum ought to, because it'll bring in some money *and* make sure people have heard of her. It's not as if she doesn't know how to teach.'

She took Sean round to the other side of the house,

through the courtyard and out to the main slope of lawn. She'd forgotten Oliver, out here with his group. He was talking to one of the students, crouching by the easel, gesturing with one hand.

'Oh – I forgot to tell you Oliver Locke's here for the weekend,' Charlie said. 'Do you want to go down and say hello?'

'I don't think so,' Sean said. 'Let's not disturb him.'

Charlie caught something in his tone. 'You don't like him, do you?'

'Not much,' Sean said.

'Why not?'

'Doesn't matter. Let's just say I don't come across him much at school, and I'm quite happy with that.'

Charlie remembered talking to Oliver under the mulberry tree, mentioning Sean; Oliver saying, 'He's one of those muscular, athletic types that makes the rest of us feel flabby and wimpish.' Charlie heard now what she hadn't at the time: sarcasm, disparagement. It had been said as a joke, but not entirely a good-natured one. Oliver had a way of turning such things into a put-down: Sean was a *type*, not a person; he was fit and sporty, therefore, Oliver's tone implied, he had no brain. If Oliver made such a remark now, she'd say something sharp in retort. She couldn't think why it had taken her so long to see through Oliver Locke.

She began to tell Sean about Kieran as they walked slowly towards the house. Then Rosie came out of the open door and ran down the grass towards them.

'Tarlie, Tarlie!' She raised her arms, wanting to be picked up.

'Rosie!' Charlie lifted her, swung her high, put her down again. 'Rosie, this is Sean.'

'Torn,' Rosie said, with the sly smile that meant she was mispronouncing on purpose. She put her head on one side and looked appealingly at Charlie. 'I want to play with *Tie*ran.'

'No, Kieran's not here today,' Charlie said. 'D'you want to come for a walk with us?'

Then she glanced at Sean.

She hadn't even thought about it. She was used to Rosie now: to the name, to Rosie herself. Even Kathy, after running away that first time, had got used to seeing her here. Charlie was tuned to her mother's loss – always trying to protect her from the hurt of a chance sighting or a misplaced word. But Rose would have been Sean's child too.

He was gazing at Rosie, his eyes shiny with tears. Charlie felt herself tingling with confusion.

'Oh God, Sean, I'm sorry,' she said. 'I didn't think.'

He didn't answer; he blinked furiously and rubbed at his eyes with a forefinger. Charlie wondered whether to give him her tissue; men never seemed to have them. Her own eyes filled with tears in sympathy as she picked Rosie up and cuddled her. Then she heard a loud, unmistakable voice from the rose garden. It declaimed: 'Of course there's such a wide interest these days that you shouldn't have trouble filling a course, and I'm sure Jiminy will step into the breach at the shop,' and Henrietta walked through the archway with Fay. It was too late to hurry away in another direction without looking rude, and anyway Charlie had Rosie in her arms. She tried to compose her face, and was about to introduce Sean to Fay when Henrietta stepped forward, getting in first.

'It's Sean, isn't it? We met before. I see you're like me, a sufferer from pollen allergy. These roses are gorgeous but they do make us pay a price for their beauty, don't they? You must come into the shop and look at my homeopathic remedies. I carry quite a range.'

'Henrietta's going to run a course on herbal healing,' Fay explained.

Charlie did the introduction. Sean, sniffy but under control, said some complimentary things about Nightingales. Fay said, 'I'll take Rosie indoors. Dan was supposed to be looking after her, but she's managed to escape. Would you like to come in for coffee?'

'Thanks, but I must be going,' Sean said.

'Let's take you back to your dad then, Miss Runaway,' Fay said to Rosie, taking her from Charlie. She and Henrietta walked on up to the house; Charlie and Sean went through to the courtyard.

'I'm sorry,' Charlie said again. 'About Rosie. I never even thought—'

'It's all right,' Sean said. 'I ought to be used to it by now, seeing other people's children, hearing about them. But every now and then it just gets me – seeing that little girl come to you, you picking her up – it's how things might have been, if—'

'Yes. I know.'

They sat on the bench. Charlie thought of the other conversations she'd had here, with Oliver, before her opinion of him had plummeted. Now, the person she most wanted to be with, the person she had longed to see, was beside her and she couldn't think of anything to say. The weight of their shared loss was heavy between them.

Then Sean said, 'I wanted to see Kathy today, as well as you.'

'Oh?'

He nodded. 'So it was lucky I found her on her own, and more approachable than usual.'

'What happened?'

Charlie stared at him, thinking: *Surely* he and Mum aren't getting together again, after he's tried so hard; not *now*.

'We talked,' Sean said. 'Properly, for the first time in ages. I told her that – I'm not going to keep pestering her any more. It's over. It's taken me a long time to realize, but at last I do.'

'Oh.'

Sean was sitting forward on the bench; he examined the splayed fingers of one hand. 'She's done better than me, in a way. She's – well, not accepted it, that's not the right word – but she's found ways to be positive. To make a new, different life. Sorting herself out, starting the gardening business – even meeting this Dietmar guy. It's not easy for her. And it's not fair if I keep trying to drag her back.'

'Don't make it sound as if you've done something wrong!'

'I don't know. Perhaps. But,' he said, looking at her, 'the one thing that's made it bearable is knowing she's got you. Otherwise I'd have been desperately worried about her. You've been fantastic.'

Charlie closed her eyes. *Please* don't tell me I'm mature and sensible, she thought: she felt anything but. With her eyes shut she felt quite dizzy. When she opened them, the rose garden reeled, like a round-about coming to a standstill.

'Are you all right?' Sean asked.

No. Seasick.

'Course,' she said. 'But what about you?'

'How d'you mean?'

'You said Mum's done better than you. Sorting her-self out. What about you?'

Sean shrugged, examining his fingers again. 'I'll be OK. I've got a job, somewhere to live, friends. Things to do.'

Charlie had a brief, silent struggle with herself. She couldn't bear to think of Sean dejected and lonely, living by himself in his flat; he deserved better. He ought to have someone to love him.

But she wasn't that person.

Disappointment and loss tugged at her, weighed heavy. It was no use fantasizing.

Sean would meet someone else, as her mother had always said. Someone his own age. Someone who was ready to have a baby. Charlie felt a surge of jealousy towards this unknown future person. But she saw that if she really loved Sean, she should be generous enough to hope that this person would turn up. Soon.

'Anyway,' Sean said. He sat back against the bench and stretched his arms above his head, as if pushing away negative thoughts. 'When I get back from Turkey we'll have another day in the Peak District, shall we? I thought next time we might—'

People coming. Loud voices: 'I mean it's perfectly obvious to me that Daphne would never dream of gossiping about such a thing, whatever Sheila may have imagined Megan meant . . .' Two women in flowered dresses, absorbed in their conversation, walked slowly into the courtyard from the archway opposite, not even noticing Charlie and Sean.

'Oh, look at the *time*,' Charlie said. The morning sessions must be over, the guests released for their pre-lunch wanderings and chat. 'I'm meant to be laying the tables. Jon will have a fit.'

'I ought to be going, too,' Sean said. 'I've got a bag of smelly clothes to take to the launderette.'

'And yes, about the Peak District,' Charlie said. 'Definitely. Please.'

She went with him to the front gate. Jon would be getting indignant in the kitchen, but instead of hurrying back she stood and watched Sean getting smaller and smaller as he walked away, about to disappear into three weeks of absence. Her eyes blurred as he reached the bend into the village and turned to wave.

That afternoon Charlie walked with her mother, Dietmar and Caspar over to the airfield. Back at Flightsend she'd found her mother and Dietmar still at the table in the garden, sharing grapes and a bottle of wine; it had been a long, leisurely lunch. Afterwards, Kathy suggested the walk.

'You come with us, Charlie. I'll put the *Closed* sign up.'

Charlie couldn't remember her mother ever doing this before at a weekend. It marked the day as special.

'Oh, by the way, Rowan phoned,' Kathy said, clipping Caspar's lead on. 'She's just got back. She wants you to play tennis one afternoon next week, with her and Russell. She thought you might ask Angus. And Angus rang, too. Not about tennis, about something else. You're in demand today.'

'But Rowan's hopeless at tennis! And Russell's brilliant, the school's number one player.'

'Angus is your Morris-dancing friend, with the hat and bells?' Dietmar asked. 'Is he a tennis-player also?'

'Yes, that's Angus. At least, he was a Morris dancer for *that* day – you never know what Angus is going to do next. He's about the same as me at tennis – that is, average but not spectacular, but there's nothing he can't have a reasonable go at – so if the two of us play Rowan and Russell it'll even out. I'll phone them both later.'

They took the shorter way to the airfield, down the footpath that led beside the Post Office, and into Hog

Pond field, soon to be transformed into Honeysuckle Coppice. The earth-diggers had moved in during the week and begun clearing part of the field. Abandoned now for the weekend like yellow beached whales, they marked the division between freshly-dug earth and the wild, untouched part of the meadow, where white butterflies hovered over the thistles and ragwort.

'Oh, it's awful,' Charlie said. 'All this'll soon disappear under concrete.'

'Charlie has secret NIMBY tendencies,' Kathy said to Dietmar. 'You know – Not In My Back Yard? Come on, Charlie, it's not that bad. It'll look a sight for a while, but when the houses are finished it won't make an awful lot of difference to the village. Hey, there'll be new gardens to be designed and planted—'

'*Mum!*' Charlie reproached. 'You're turning into a hard-headed businesswoman! Never mind the destruction of the environment – all you see is a career opportunity!'

'Besides,' Dietmar said, 'it looks as if this field has been furrow.'

'No, I think you mean . . .' Charlie knew that *furrow* wasn't the right word, but couldn't think what was.

'Furrow? You mean after it's been ploughed up?' Kathy said. 'No, I don't think it's been ploughed for ages.'

Dietmar stopped, frowning. 'No. Farrow. That's what I meant.'

'But farrowing is to do with pigs,' Charlie said. 'It's when a pig has piglets. You say a pig has farrowed,

237

don't you? That's right, isn't it, Mum?'

'No, I wasn't meaning pigs,' Dietmar said. 'Even though you say this field is named Hog Pond.'

'*Harrow*,' Kathy said. 'That's when they trail a sort of wiry or discy thing over the ground, to break up clods. And you say something was a *harrowing experience.*'

Dietmar still wasn't satisfied, shaking his head, puzzled.

'Got it!' Charlie said. '*Fallow.* The field's been lying fallow. It hasn't had anything grown in it.'

'Yes! Thank you, Charlie. That is what I meant to say. If the field is fallow and not used for farming, then a few houses are perhaps a reasonable use. But *fallow* is also deer, I think?'

'Yes, it is. Fallow deer. Furrow, farrow, harrow, fallow – no wonder we're in a muddle,' Kathy said, laughing. 'It's a tongue-twister!'

'Tongue-twister?' Dietmar queried. 'A twisting of the tongue, to say something very difficult, yes?'

'That's right.'

'All these words so similar. Now German is such a simple, straightforward language.'

They reached the stile and climbed over into the airfield. Dietmar walked straight to his father's cross and they all stood there for a few moments. Charlie thought: people were here, doing their jobs, watching from the control tower, while it happened – the aircraft burst into flames and Dietmar's father burned to death within a few metres of people who'd have saved him if they could. Even though he was enemy. His mission, Dietmar had told her, was to destroy the bomber planes on the ground. Instead, his own plane had been destroyed, and him with it. She was surprised and moved by Dietmar's attachment to the father he'd never known; Dietmar had followed him not only to the place of death but also into the sky, in the Cessna. If the airfield ever *were* taken over for a housing development, she thought, at least the story had come to light. It wouldn't be lost, churned up by the earth-movers and dug into the ground.

'All those years ago, I could not have stood here like this,' Dietmar said, breaking the silence. 'A German. I would have been interrogated as a spy and clapped into an internment camp.'

'And yet you came to live here,' Kathy said.

'Yes. But now I feel more at home here than I did then. In the village, and at Flightsend. Perhaps, now,' he said, looking at Kathy, 'the name really means what I wished for.'

Flight's End.

Charlie understood that with this remark Dietmar had said something rather wonderful to her mother. She also remembered Kathy's words when they first saw the cottage: 'That's what it is, isn't it? An end to everything that's gone wrong.' And she had made it so, in her own way, with determination and courage. Not the way Charlie would have chosen, but nevertheless it was working.

They walked on, Dietmar and Kathy hand-in-hand.

Pretending not to notice, Charlie knew that her mother, if challenged, would say that they were just good friends.

Why do people say that, she wondered? What's *just* about a good friend?

She thought of Sean, who'd send her postcards from Turkey, who'd come back and take her to the Peak District; who'd remain her friend, though he didn't have to. She thought of Rowan and Angus. Her friends. She'd see them soon.

Caspar scouted ahead, nose to the ground, tail high. Although the airfield was only slightly higher than the village, Charlie had the feeling of being above everything, distanced in the strange timelessness of the perimeter tracks and runways. The church tower was squatly huddled into its yew trees, the houses packed close around the green. The day had turned cool, a breeze ruffling the grasses. In the triangles cut by the runways, the barley crop had been harvested, leaving the ground dry and stalky. Swallows skimmed low.

'Swallows, or house martins?' Kathy said. 'I always forget how to tell the difference.'

'They're swallows,' Charlie said. She knew because Sean knew. 'They've got a reddish bit under their throat. House martins have white rumps and shorter tails.'

'Martin is also a small animal, like a polecat?' Dietmar asked, and they were off again, sorting their way through words and meanings.

'Marten, *E* – N. As in pine marten,' Kathy said.

Charlie walked ahead, letting them talk. She whistled Caspar and he waited, turning to grin over his shoulder. She was amazed by her own mood swing. Not three hours ago, when Sean left, she could have hidden in the toilet and wept for the end of her silly flight of fantasy. But now she saw that it had been replaced by something better and stronger. She thought of all she had to look forward to: the flight in the Cessna next Saturday, and seeing Rowan, and tennis with Angus; Sean coming back, and the start of the sixth form. Even getting the exam results in two weeks' time was probably something she could look forward to, rather than dread.

'Come on, Caspar!' She picked up a stick and hurled it for him. She loved to see him galloping fast, stretched out like a cheetah in a surge of pure speed that was thrilling to watch. She ran after him without a hope of keeping up. He caught the stick, pinned it to the ground with a forepaw and fastened his jaws round it, then trotted back to her.

'Good boy!' She hurled it again, watched him leap, capture and tussle. She was on the main runway now, at the highest part of the airfield, with Dietmar and her mother walking slowly towards her. From here she could see the dipping, weathered roof of Flightsend itself, beyond the church yews.

It was still August, but the landscape was taking on the mature colours of autumn. Clusters of elderberries were forming on wine-red stems; the rowan in the hedge was decked with orange berries. Charlie thought of autumn: of misty, cobwebby mornings, of long shadows, of bonfires and Hallowe'en. Things would happen in their proper order.

She looked down at Flightsend. She thought of the table in the garden, with the remains of lunch. Her mother's rows of labelled plants in the nursery, the seedlings and cuttings, the smell of fertile, watered earth. Frühlingsmorgen in the garden, soon to be joined by Rose's rose. Her own bedroom, with its clutter and its secrets and its window overlooking the garden and meadows.

Home.

Also by Linda Newbery

THE
SHELL HOUSE
By LINDA NEWBERY

When Greg stumbles across the beautiful ruins of
Graveney Hall, he becomes intrigued by the story behind
its destruction. He and his friend Faith are drawn into
a quest to discover the fate of Graveney's last
heir, Edmund, a young soldier who disappeared in
mysterious circumstances during the First World War.

But Greg's investigations force him to question his own
views on love and faith, and reveal more about
himself than he would ever have imagined.

SHORTLISTED FOR THE CARNEGIE MEDAL AND
THE GUARDIAN CHILDREN'S FICTION PRIZE

978 0 099 45593 6

SISTERLAND
By LINDA NEWBERY

*If I had a choice – know, or not know – I'd have to
choose knowing. It must
always be better to know, mustn't it?*

When Heidigran comes to live with the Craig
family, her granddaughter Hilly finds that events
buried in the past can deeply affect the
present. As Heidigran becomes increasingly ill and
confused, secrets are unveiled which threaten to
rock the stability of the whole family.
What impact will revelations of her wartime
experiences have on Hilly's sense of identity?

978 0 099 47282 7

SET IN STONE

By LINDA NEWBERY

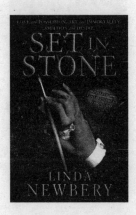

When naïve and impressionable artist, Samuel Godwin,
accepts the position of tutor to the daughters of
wealthy Ernest Farrow, he does not suspect that he's
walking into a web of deception. He is drawn into the
lives of three young women: Charlotte Agnew, the
governess; demure Juliana, the elder daughter, and her
passionate and wilful younger sister, Marianne, who
intrigues Samuel to the point of obsession.

And it's not just the people who entrance Samuel.
The house, Fourwinds, holds mysteries of its own,
and soon Samuel and Charlotte start to uncover
horrifying and dangerous secrets . . .

978 0 099 45133 4